# Ekleipsis

## In the Land of Erde

Pordlaw mit LaRue

Copyright © 2007

By

Pordlaw mit LaRue


Cover Art

By

Pordlaw LaRue & Sean Labat


Paperback Edition

ISBN: 978-0-6151-8434-0


www.landoferde.com

# Contents

Acknowledgements ..................................................... 5

Dedication ............................................................. 7

**Book One:**
**Ekleipsis**
**9**

To Begin At a Moment ............................................. 13

A History of Sorts .................................................... 15

Return to the Moment ............................................... 25

Spring Forward a Little ............................................. 31

Old Enough For a Gift .............................................. 39

Turning Points in History .......................................... 43

A Glance into Darkness ............................................ 51

A Goodbye to Remember .......................................... 55

Joys for the Moment ................................................ 61

Desire for the Supernatural ........................................ 67

Trachten, Land of the Seekers .................................... 75

Choices ............................................................... 87

Hope in Signum .................................................... 95

Secrets Revealed ................................................... 103

Insight and Understanding ........................................ 117

**Meeting of the Gibborims** .......................................... 133

**Hozekan Warning** .................................................. 141

**Unrest in the Land of Erde** ...................................... 149

    *Trachten* .................................................... 149

    *Signum* ...................................................... 152

    *Nesal* ....................................................... 155

**Separated Hearts** ................................................. 159

**Rally in Geheim** .................................................. 163

**Ekleipsis** ........................................................ 169

Book Two Preview:
Daegsteorra
173

**APPENDIX** ......................................................... 177

    *Characters* .................................................. 179

    *Groups* ...................................................... 185

    *Places* ...................................................... 187

    *Hidden Meanings* ............................................. 191

        *The List* ............................................ 191

        *The Light* ........................................... 195

        *The Darkness* ........................................ 197

About the Author
199

# Acknowledgements

I would like to personally thank the editorial eyes and thoughts, along with constructional criticism and ideas, from the following:

Family & Friends

Elizabeth, Judy, Stephen, & Rebecca Waldrop
Sean Labat

Friend & Editor

Evelyn Huckaby

I appreciate your time, effort, and willingness to help and give advice to a novice writer with dreams, asking nothing in return.

With my deepest gratitude, I say,

Thank you.

# Dedication

To all that have suffered persecution in one form or another, to those that have sacrificed that others may have, and to those that one day may be called upon to do the same.

Never lose faith!

# Book One:

## In the Land of Erde

*Ekleipsis* (Greek, *eclipse*): Judarius claimed that darkness would one day overcome and destroy all light. The name of that day, he called thus.

# To Begin At a Moment

I t is a cold, stormy night in the midst of a small village, one seemingly lost from the world among the mountains and valleys of a nameless place, full of forgotten souls. Howling winds blow wildly through the large trees that surround the village, protecting it like a great wall around a castle. The streets are empty of souls, where only debris flies effortlessly on the breath of the night. Hoping for a brighter tomorrow, families snuggle in bed resisting the fear that creeps among the shadows waiting to gain entrance into the mind that dares to embrace it.

These storms seem to come forth from the mountains most unaware to the people below. Sometimes ceasing as quickly as they had come, other times lingering well for hours without losing strength. Attacking with the force of a mighty army, the bitter winds slice through the thickest clothing, chapping faces, and reddening exposed flesh. The heavens send forth hardened crystals upon all caught beneath the clouds, often simply melting away into the sodden paths.

Through the gloom, a small home near the edge of the village remains alive, entertaining the dancing of lantern lights and the patter of footsteps. *Why tonight? Why must it be during a time of such disarray?* A small, elderly lady with silver-laced hair flowing to her waist paces the floor running to and fro, ministering to a young girl slightly above her teens.

*Dear God, I pray that you show compassion. Hear the frail attempt of your child to call upon such a mighty God to request such a selfish thing as this. Lend your ear to my pleading and see what is right in your own eyes. Thou hast given Sorie life and have been gracious to spring forth life from within her womb. Shall she carry such a love only to perish at its coming? Do as thou see fit, but remember compassion. In thee will I trust to do that which is right.*

Sorie is due any minute with delivery, yet boiling with fever she feels her life slipping ever so slowly away. Her brown hair, tangled and glued to her face with beads of sweat, hides well the beauty she possesses. Hardly able to hold her eyes open, fading in and out of consciousness, there is but one thought which grips the entire essence of her being: *How is my baby?*

For the last nine months she could think of nothing else than the soul which has grown within her. She caressed her stomach often and longed to see the face of her child. As those which she knew would speak of their own, her lightly tanned face would glow as her brown eyes sparkled with eagerness of what was to come. She delighted in the stories of others, and hoped to the uttermost that she would be a good mother to such a lovely gift.

# A History of Sorts

*F*rom the beginning, Sorie had a fondness for a young tan lad by the name of Tindal. Tindal, though rather small in stature, was fearless. Somewhat defined, though not overly muscular, he was the son of his athletic father MaZak. Hairless from birth, Tindal would often be mocked by the other boys, who soon learned to keep their comments to themselves or in secret.

Tindal was very smart and loved history. He would often spend hours in the makeshift library reading books on all types of topics. He enjoyed comparing the different perspectives of various authors' writings of the same time and subjects. Tindal could never read enough, as he would audibly agree and disagree with various writers, full of passion when it came to the law and history of Erde, whether it would be of King Salvare and the *Sealed*, or the *Darkness*.

Tindal's father, MaZak, had brought books from his days at Kirche, the school where the *Sealed* are trained. Others which sometimes visited the markets in Trachten would also purchase a variety of books to share with all in the communal library in Nesal. Although MaZak did not agree with the content of all the books, they were there none the least. Men would read that which they wished, and he could not be every man's conscience.

Tindal's father was a well-defined swordsman. He was known throughout the lands as *The Bladesman*. He was considered to be, if not the best, one of the best sword makers and carriers around. MaZak had chosen to move to Nesal for the purpose of removing him and his family from the mainstream of things. Although he had served the *Sealed* well for many years, he now desired to keep his family far from the deceits of the *Darkness* due south and the mere gossip within the limits of Signum at Kirche, which now burdened his heart.

Nesal is a small valley hidden by the Cadas Mountains and Lake Szikla to its north and east, with large oaks and sycamores of the Ascuns Forest to its south and west. It is a quiet and peaceful place out of sight and mind of most in the land of Erde. Most prefer the large, busy spaces of Erde, while some still hold to the peaceful sounds of calmness from the crowds.

He felt that he could enjoy his wife and raise his family away from all the problems of the world by hiding away. He had seen too much he wished to keep from his family. He cared not that he would have to leave the luxuries of the modern large village of Signum, due north west from Nesal, where Kirche is. It is in the quiet of Nesal MaZak felt his family could better hear the voice of God, and ponder the words of the *Book of Wisdom* from King Salvare.

Twice a year MaZak traveled to the Land of the *Seekers*, which set up markets to have those from around the land of Erde bring new and interesting creations to buy, sell, and trade. Men of dignity and power sometimes send their servants from far kingdoms to have *The Bladesman* handcraft each minute detail into the finest metals to become weapons of war and protection. And on occasion, some dignitaries pay a personal visit just to view and offer a price to his prized possession, *Reflection*.

MaZak named his most famous piece of work, *Reflection*, for two reasons, or so he said. The first was due to the nature of his work; his swords were created to hold the smoothest, shiniest reflection even after a day's worth of battle. As for the second, which he most often enjoyed to tell, if it were true that man indeed saw his life flash before his eyes at the very moment of death, then very well it was the *Reflection* which brought him face to face with it.

MaZak was a gracious man and full of wisdom. Strong as an ox and built like red cedar, none dare cross him, but underneath was a man of compassion with a soft touch for his wife and child. He taught them the way of the *Sealed* and spoke often of the *Shimmering* kingdom. Numbered among the *Sealed* himself, he long served the true *King*, Salvare, valiantly along the frontlines and as a craftsman for the better part of his life. He had recently removed himself from the frontlines, moving to Nesal to spend his time defining works of art, namely swords. He claimed the frontlines were for the young to fight fervent and fierce, while it was the old one's duty to lend support through teaching and training.

"One cannot fight forever, for no man's light is eternally lit in this life, but our knowledge and swords may be passed down from generation unto generation; for the battles against the *Shadow Lands* and the kingdom of *Darkness* shall continue to rage on long after we are gone. Fight while you are able, that others may be protected. Hold on to faith in times of doubt, to give encouragement to the weak. Live life by the law, so others may know what is right. Give honor and show compassion, that others may want to follow. Remember your testimony as to the kingdom, as you serve, in all obedience, Salvare, the true *King*, that the world may know that he is righteous, pure at heart, is yet alive, and has a love for people. Let not King Salvare return to see us standing idle in the streets as those around us are slain in the name of the *Wicked One*. Become one with your sword and wear the *King's* armor proudly. Fight for Truth! Long live the *King!*" From his farewell address given to the youth who much enjoyed his stories, he said goodbye to a life of battle, but not of service.

Tindal's mother, Eslar, was much in love with her soldier, MaZak. He had rescued her from the *Shadow Lands* and told her of King Salvare. Although he would never take credit for saving her from such, he told her it was the *King's Whisper* that indeed had led him to her and had awakened her from the *Shadows*.

§     §     §     §

The *Shadow Lands* are where many a soul drifts away, never to be seen or heard from again. It is a veil whereby the wickedness may pass between the light of Erde and the *Darkness* of *Oscuridad*. There be those who have lost themselves among the thick fog of the *Shadows* in search of the *Darkness*, but most have been taken captive by the *Darkness* itself. Being brought there, hearts soon become burdened beyond measure, their minds confounded by the wickedness which dwells therein, their bodies worn by the unhealthy conditions of the climate, and soon all hope is lost as the *Darkness* overcomes them. Some souls are saved from such, being pulled from the bonds of the *Darkness* back into the glorious light of the sun, nourished by those which fight against the *Darkness* and serve the true *King*. Of such a one was Eslar.

§     §     §     §

Day after day, as he spoke of the *King* and the *Shimmering* kingdom, she longed the more to see it and to meet this great *King* of which he spoke. He told her that one day soon, King Salvare would indeed return with his kingdom and that she would then be able to behold him face to face, but until then, one's faith must rest in the work of the *King* and his words, "Fear not my children, I shall return to you my people." So she did.

Even from her youth, this lady looked small and frail, but was very much a hard worker and quite feisty when the situation called for it. Ever striving to please him, never had she felt such love from any other man. She had neither known her father nor mother, but was an orphan, which most seemed to over look. She would often claim, "When one has been pulled from the

*Shadows*, what are the trials of life but a small thing."

If there were days she would consider the greatest of all in her life, she would say it was the day she was saved from the *Shadows*, the meeting of her love, and the birth of her only son Tindal.

Tindal was a most disciplined young man. He would anxiously await the arrival of his father and beg him to tell him the stories again and again - though he had heard them many times before - of how King Salvare had come, was betrayed by a friend, and was slain by kindred and those that serve the *Darkness*, yet rose again by the power of his father Allmachtig, and promised to return to gather his people unto his *Shimmering* kingdom, called *Scimerian*.

§   §   §   §

*Scimerian*, the *Shimmering* kingdom, is described by King Salvare himself in the *Book of Wisdom*. "My children, behold when I shall return, to henceforth destroy the darkness forevermore, I shall bring you forth to New Erde as Erde shall be no more. Even now do I go away to prepare such a place for you. As you approach ye shall see the gates to the great *Shimmering* kingdom, *Scimerian*, overlade with precious stones, which shall never be closed. Ye shall enter upon streets of purest gold, able to be traveled by foot, for they are soft and pleasurable to walk upon. The vegetation shall cover the ground as a blanket, with colors so beautiful to behold, one can feel the warmth of their color. The trees stretch forth their arms, full of ripened, bountiful fruit, toward the bright sun which casts its light, forbidding forever the shadows and darkness entrance. There shall be no more sorrow among the gates of *Scimerian* within New Erde, for my desire is for your hearts to be pure and full of joy. Ye shall behold me as your king, and I shall love you as my people forever."

§   §   §   §

He would carefully listen as his father would read the law and tell his father that he would be the first to keep that law perfectly, so the *King* would know he loved him.

MaZak would chuckle and say, "Dear Tindal, do not fear if you by chance falter or stumble at the law. Indeed it is right to desire to obey without error, but the law is not what allows you into the kingdom; the *King* himself must grant you entrance."

"Aye, father, but how much more so shall the *King* accept that one which is perfect?"

Sorie's family on the other hand, had been slaughtered by an attack of the servants of the kingdom of *Darkness*, called *Oscuridad*, as they overtook Almozak, where she lived. As the *Gottlos* attacked, strong delusions overwhelmed the people of the village, causing them to slay one another 'midst the battle. It was as though the people had been controlled by another, having them do things they normally would not.

§ § § §

The *Darkness* is that which some believe has always been, though others consider began with the treason of Judarius. Dwelling along the south west outskirts of Erde, though close enough to touch it, the *Shadows Lands* are all that appear to separate *Oscuridad* and Erde. Those which fall into the *Darkness*, such as the *Gottlos*, never again return to the light except to fight against it. The *Darkness* and the servants thereof merely wait eagerly among the shadows throughout Erde, to overcome the soul which knows not their devices.

§ § § §

There were no survivors, save Sorie. The village was left desolate with the bodies of those dead, lingering where they lay in the streets and homes, as the *Gottlos* left as quickly as they had come, snickering and laughing with delight in what they had done to those people who were unaware. Though rebuilt, Sorie had never returned.

Was it by chance or something more that young Sorie had been saved from such torture as that? (To this day she ponders why the entire village had to perish, save her. She still misses her family, but is no longer angered by it.) She had returned from visiting her cousin Tamar in Felter, to find the village and all she had burning. Her joy was stolen by sadness.

As the smoke pushed its way through the fresh breeze, it carried the smell of death and sorrow like a message to others that may also fall prey to the desires of the *Gottlos*, the servants of *Darkness*. The stench of the smoldering bodies was horrendous, along with the ashes carried by the wind, which caused her eyes to burn. These were people she knew, people she loved.

Sorie stood there in fright, yet amazed. Wanting to turn away, but unable, her tears found themselves watering the grass beneath her feet. If only she had not gone to visit Tamar, though she may have died, she would still be with her family.

*How could such have happened? Have they all perished? Am I but left? Shall I call to them only to hear the crackling of the fire 'midst the ashes that remain?*

Sorie stood alone as time seemed to stand still, and she scarcely heard the thunder of hooves quickly approaching from behind her. An average-sized bearded man wearing a tan cloak, carrying a strait smooth wooden staff, approached and placed his hand upon her shoulder. Odd, it was comforting, as if known.

Her lips drew fierce, "Where then are the *King* and the *Sealed*? Have they no desire for the peasants of the land? Are we but nothing in their eyes? Have you come now but to scoff?" She was fifteen years old, but not some silly child of adolescence.

The man who held her was Ashvar, a *seer*[f] among the *Sealed*. He explained that indeed, the village leaders had been told of the coming threat many moons ago, but had played the spoiled child choosing not to heed the warnings. Ashvar softly explained that although the *Sealed* had desired to enlighten and move the villagers to a safer location, King Salvare's words had always been clear that they were not to force people into protection, but to persuade through words of wisdom. It was odd, but she trusted the words of this unknown man. With no family or place to go, Ashvar took Sorie home with him. From that day, he beheld her as daughter, and she loved him as father.

It was in the Land of the *Seekers* at the semiannual market that Sorie first laid eyes on Tindal. Instantly there was a strange attraction between the two. From that day they became inseparable. Were they meant to be together or was it that neither had found another to take interest in? Neither cared for such foolish questions; they were young and in love, having eyes for only one another.

A few years later they made vows to one another to be faithful and chose to marry. They chose to live in the village of Nesal with Tindal's family, but were not too far from Breckenly, the village of her adoptive father Ashvar. Things were going well for them, as their relationship developed from young love to couple charity; the love which brings forth both action and commitment, above and beyond the youthful lust of initial sight.

Tindal had chosen a life of knowledge and learning over following in his father's footsteps of the craftsmanship of swords. At the first, MaZak wanted much to persuade his son to embrace the skill of the swordsman, but soon gave in to the idea that his son was more involved in learning and studies. It somewhat disheartened MaZak to acknowledge Tindal's lack of want toward

---

[f] able to see and proclaim the future (receives ability from God, contrasted to a pale)

his talents, but recalled how if his mother would have had her way, he would have been a shepherd instead of *The Bladesman*, wishing to keep him away from the dangers of being numbered among the *Sealed*.

Tindal desired to be a Master of the law and study of not only the *King* and the kingdom, but also of the *Gottlos* and of the history of *Oscuridad*. MaZak warned against such peering into the hidden thoughts of the kingdom of *Darkness*, but Tindal would not heed his father's words. MaZak knew he could have demanded obedience, but Tindal would have merely found time to fulfill his desires of such studies in secret.

MaZak had told Tindal an overabundance of law study would lead to a legalistic view that could cause one to be blind to grace and mercy, and an exhausted study of history could lead to a lack of desire to act, feeling it had all been tried before. Even as taking the *Book of Wisdom* out of context, for King Salvare had promised to return, could cause one to be lazy waiting on the *King*. MaZak also knew peering too deeply into the *Darkness* was not good for a man's soul.

Soon after marriage, Sorie told Tindal she was with child. He was excited and began to plan out their entire future together. Little did he know that his plans did not include what would one day take precedence in his life, nor was he prepared, yet though he thought.

Life is a journey, and though a man plan for the future, he cannot prepare for that which he knoweth not of.

# Return to the Moment

With a loud thump the door flew open as the wind threw it against the wall. Two men rushed into the home as the rain soared through the doorway as locusts. Eslar turned in fright as the fresh bowl of water in her hands fell to the ground. She froze still. At the noise the men jerked to face her. Pottery and water covered the floor.

Rushing over to her with his arms stretched forth, one said, "I have the doctor Eslar. Are you okay?"

"Yes MaZak, you startled me," Eslar replied excitedly.

"Has Tindal returned yet?" MaZak asked as Dr. Toggle pushed the door closed against the weather.

"Not yet. Please Dr. Toggle, see to Sorie as I clean up this mess. She is boiling with unquenchable fever."

The doctor moved around the spilt water into the bedroom with Sorie and closed the door behind him. MaZak grabbed a towel to help Eslar soak up the water and pick up the large pieces of broken pottery.

Within the space of half an hour, two more men arrived at the home. Fighting against the weather, they entered and locked the door behind them. They were soaking wet.

MaZak stood to greet them, "Tindal. Ashvar. Dr. Toggle is here, the time of birth is upon us, but her fever will not fade."

Tindal felt his blood carry the uncertainty of what was next throughout his body. He removed his drenched poncho, and Ashvar took off his saturated cloak.

"Fear not, Sorie shall live to see her child," claimed Ashvar most assuredly.

Ashvar's eyes were fixed with truth, and his voice quivered not. Neither questioned the *seer*, but both held still the slightest seed of unbelief. Never had any known Ashvar to lie, for he was one who was close to God, but faith easily wavers in times of suffering and worry.


Ashvar made his way to the room and Eslar followed, closing the door behind them. Dr. Toggle stood over Sorie checking her vitals and assessing her condition. Patting her face lightly with the damp cloth, he feared there was nothing he could do. Looking up from Sorie's pale face, seeing Ashvar, he stepped aside. He knew Sorie was in need of a greater physician than he, if both she and the child were to live.

As if Eslar and Dr. Toggle were not present, Ashvar moved around to the head of the bed. One could hear the sloshing of his wet robe against the floor as he walked toward Sorie. Kneeling beside her, he placed his left hand over her brow, placing his other atop her right hand. He bowed his head as the room was still.

Ashvar spoke with his heart to God, with words not audible for man to hear. He is a man of prayer, one who communes with God. Prepared from the womb of his mother, raised in the nurture and admonition of the Lord, he has always been a *seer* and friend of the Most High.

Moments that seemed like hours passed by. Afraid to move, Eslar and Dr. Toggle watched as the *seer* knelt in silence with his eyes closed. Eslar cried in her spirit for God to grant healing, as Dr. Toggle offered his own prayers to the Father.

MaZak and Tindal remained outside the room, knowing there was nothing they could do to help. Helplessness is not one's favorite state to be found in, but few there be which escape it. Fighting for prominence, fear and faith mixed with prayers filled their minds as they waited. They could not deny the doubt which desired to overwhelm them, but they fought against giving it precedence over all else in their being.

MaZak kneeled, hunched over the seat of the wooden chair in the corner of the living area. Across the room in the kitchen, where the bowl and water had been cleaned up, Tindal sat with his eyes staring at the floor between his legs. The sounds of the storm could still be heard through the small cracks around the windows and door. As MaZak sent up prayers to heaven, Tindal's mind was full of small repetitious prayers of, "please help Sorie and the baby" over and over again.

Ashvar lifted himself from the ground. Bending over, he gently kissed Sorie upon her forehead and turned toward the others. "God has seen it fit to remove the fever. The time is at hand. She is ready to deliver."

Sorie's eyes faintly opened as faith was instantly renewed in the room. Color slowly filled her cheeks once more. The baby was coming as the doctor began his work. Washing his hands, Dr. Toggle prepared for the child's deliverance. Eslar was there to help with towels and fresh water, as Ashvar made his way out the door to be with MaZak and Tindal.

Eslar touched the face of Sorie as she looked into her eyes, allowing Sorie to squeeze her other hand. Sorie's skin was cool, no longer burning with fever. *It's a miracle*, Eslar conceded, *a marvelous miracle indeed.* Sorie puffed and blew trying to make herself take deep breaths and excel fully, as she pushed with each contraction.

Little Vandor was about to flow from darkness to light, from the womb into the land of Erde. Today he would be born among the dark howls of the night storm, but tomorrow he would feel the warmth of the bright sun upon his tender skin. From the safety of his mother's womb, he would soon be among the forces of good and evil.

Sorie anticipated the precious smile of her son, which somewhat eased the discomforts of her groans and cries through the pain of birth. Dr. Toggle, with his sleeves rolled up and freshly washed hands, held the newborn. With a fresh damp cloth, Dr. Toggle cleaned out the eyes, ears, and mouth of the child. A small cry and then another. New life: a beginning with opportunity and promise for both failure and success, a desire for wants and a need for understanding, a blessing and a gift.

No one cared for the disarray among the wind and rain of the night; a baby was born, new life had sprung forth. Cheers and tears filled the home. Burdens lifted, fears released, prayers answered; it appeared mercy had been granted. The small room, where moments ago were filled with silence, was now full of family and laughter.

Sorie, exhausted, beheld her child with sleepy eyes, "My little Vandor Leshing."

A bond, that which a mother instinctively feels for her baby, was made without thought. She held him close, wrapped in a soft blue blanket covering his body and head, only revealing the face and arms. His eyes squinted against the light, with the faintest hint of eyebrows.

Tindal gazed at his son; small and new to this world. Countless things passed through his mind as he took in every bit of baby Vandor; things that must be done, things that must be taught, what to be expected. *Does not every father ponder these things within his heart*, he wonders.

"Shall we dedicate him to God and the *King*, as it is written in the *Book of Wisdom* Ashvar?" asked Tindal.

"If you and Sorie be agreed, then so be it," replied Ashvar.

"We are, let it be so," claimed Tindal.

"Yes, father, we would like as much to be done," agreed Sorie faintly, still looking ever so tenderly at her newborn.

She lightly kissed Vandor and lifted him toward Ashvar. Vandor's eyes were wide open as if taking in all that was new. MaZak and Eslar stood near the door anxious to hold the child, but patiently waited their due turn. This was a moment of dedication, an important moment indeed. A picture whereby the parents offer their precious gift of life back to God, which saw it fit to grant them as an inheritance.

Ashvar stepped up to the bed and took the child from his mother's arms. Lifting him up in front of his chest as if to hand him over to another, he began to speak: "Dear young Vandor, before knowing good or evil, thy parents doth dedicate thee to the great and holy God, thy Creator. It is He who has seen it right to grant thee life, and to Him doth thou eternally owe it. To the law may thou be obedient, love God, and serve the *King* with diligence; honor thy father and mother that thy days may be long; take heed to godly wisdom from those which prove to be wise; strive to give light to those in darkness; give service to those around thee, thy kindred and thy neighbor; shun the teachings and babblings of the kingdom of *Darkness* and the servants thereof; in all things keep thyself pure, for we know one shall reap from what is sown. Long live the *King* and long may thou serve him in pure of heart. To God be all the honor, glory, and praise forevermore. Amen."

# Spring Forward a Little

"Come on Kayla. Let's go to my grandfather's shop and see what he is working on," begged Vandor as he walked by seeing Kayla out front sitting in the flowers. She was a true flower child, for she dwelt among them always as if they were her very family.

"Yes Vandor, but give me a moment. I must tell mother before she frets," replied Kayla running into her house.

§ § § §

Now thirteen, Vandor met Kayla when they were about seven. Her family lived in Felter, near Trachten, where Tamar, Sorie's cousin lives. For fear of the *Gottlos* and all the people during the times of the market, they chose to move. When they arrived here in Nesal and found that some of the *Sealed* actually dwelt here, they decided to stay.

Not to be confused with the *Masonisti*, which often dabble in secrets, the *Sealed* were formed for the open proclamation of the *Truth* as pronounced by King Salvare through his *Book of Wisdom*, and for the protection of the people from the servants of *Darkness*.

The *Masonisti* claim to be a secret sect of the *Sealed*, but there are no references to them in the *Book of Wisdom* by King Salvare, nor in any of the writings of the men which held the office of Auctoritas, nor in any of the records of the meetings of the Council of Kirche. And they are so secret, that which may be known of them, is not by any *Sealed* or non-*Sealed* outside of the *Masonisti* covenant.

The first time Vandor saw Kayla was at his grandfather's shop. She appeared very shy as she hung on her father's leg while he spoke to MaZak. Vandor instantly took a liking to her. She had delicate features with a hint of tomboy. She smiled at him, as he stood there covered in dirt from head to toe, and that settled their friendship with him then and there.

The family was new in the village and stopped by to hear MaZak tell the stories he often told of the *King*, the *Shimmering* kingdom, and the battles in which he had once taken part. Not to mention the swords and such he had for sale. Children love stories, and so do most adults.

Many would often stop by just to see his artwork engraved in the shiny blades of craftsmanship, not to mention *Reflection*. There was probably only one in a hundred or more that could match his quality of work. He was a hidden legend, one well known as *The Bladesman* of the *Sealed* of Erde, but few knew he dwelt in Nesal.

Kayla's father, Tebad, had a sword he had found that was old, which was dull, twisted, and held not a shine. He had heard that *The Bladesman* may be able to repair such a weapon, but if not, surely had such that were ten times its worth. MaZak had told him that it wasn't worth the repairs because of the material from which it had been forged. Tebad told MaZak he could keep the sword and would think of purchasing one for himself soon.

§    §    §    §

Vandor and Kayla ran as fast as they could, racing down the dirt path to MaZak's workshop in the middle of the village. Their hearts pounding and lungs trying to keep up, they embraced the feel of adrenaline pumping through their bodies and the wind against their faces.

Panting as they ran, "You're slow for a boy," laughed Kayla.

Struggling to catch his breath, Vandor smiled, "Hold your tongue woman!"

Giggling, they continued neck and neck down the way. Coming to a stop, which was most likely a tie, neither would claim the other the victor. Bent over, with their hands holding their sides, they paused to catch their breath, each looking at the other, with their redden cheeks, grinning between exhales.

MaZak was currently helping someone, so Vandor reached for two old swords his grandfather had, sitting among others in the trash bin of unused, broken, and damaged metals. This was their arsenal, full of antique relics that had once been in the hands of various persons across all of Erde. Their imaginations easily turned these remnants of forgotten possessions into the finest designed weaponry of the *King*.

Ting! Ting! Back and forth they would go dueling to the death, or at least lunch time. Laughing, they enjoyed each other's company. Best friends to the fullest, they were nearly never seen apart. If they were, be sure the other was but minutes away and would be along shortly. Vandor saw Kayla as such an interesting one, for she could be the most delicate girl whom sits among the flowers singing, yet fight him using the sword as well as any boy.

From behind Vandor came a small figure from the shadows. Moving precisely, it quickly dashed toward him. Kayla's eyes widen as she paused for a split second. Vandor, unaware as to why Kayla paused, seized the opportunity, and went in for the strike.

"Vandor – behind you," Kayla cried, as she took a step back.

Too late! Vandor slightly turned, only to be met with arms gripping around his waist and the weight of another pushing him forward toward the ground. He was struck in the back with the brute force of adrenalin.

"Huh!" His sword propelled from his hand as he reached to break the fall into the dirt. Vandor's forearms slowed his fall, before his face rested upon the ground. He collapsed with the impact of the unknown attacker upon his back and a puff of dust settling on his face, with his eyes shut and mouth puckered like he was sucking on lemons.

Heart pounding, Kayla ran forward with the sword tightly gripped in her hand. "Ye shall die ye wicked servant," as she pointed her sword toward the attacker's back. "Release him or taste death by the sword of the *King*," she claimed. "Beg for mercy, if by chance I choose to grant thee pardon of life for such a traitorous act. Release him or become as one that goest down into the pit, never to rise again."

"Hahaha - You are too much the part Kayla," claimed the attacker. "You were easily taken Vandor – Hahaha."

"Ah, get off me Rayhold, you crazy goof," puffed Vandor through the dirt in his mouth. He was not at all amused by the grit he now had amidst his teeth, so soon before lunch. He would indeed return the favor at the most opportune time.

§     §     §     §

Friends for quite some time, Vandor and Rayhold seldom ceased from getting the best of one another. Slightly taller, Vandor would most often claim the advantage, so Rayhold relied on his stealth to avenge himself. Easily would one take hold of the other for fun, but let not a stranger come betwixt the two; ah, or the three of such young people.

Rayhold was of a darker shade tan than Vandor and olive Kayla. His eyes were pitch black, which varied from Vandor's hazy brown and Kayla's emerald green. His head was as slick and shiny as Vandor's father Tindal, whereas Vandor's was simple, short and brown, with Kayla's long and auburn. These three were a true variety of subjects, yet saw nothing but friendship in one another.

Rayhold's father, Labo, handcrafted all types of leather and his mother, Sycress, was a maker of fine linen. They had once lived in the Land of the *Seekers* in Telbaton, but claimed to have moved due to the high traffic of people which passed through there because of the markets and such. They were quiet people, seldom seen or heard, which performed most of their trading outside of Nesal.

§　　§　　§　　§

It was now lunch time and these three were hungry. They thoroughly enjoyed eating with MaZak, as he always seemed to have a new and exciting story to tell. Sometimes he would actually tell the same story with a different perspective which made it seem new and exciting. Living among the inhabitants of Signum and numbered among the *Sealed* for so long, he had plenty of stories for the children to hear. There were also the stories passed down from his father, along with his incorporation of many of the writings of the *Book of Wisdom* into most all of his tellings.

Vandor looked at the old twisted sword Kayla still held in her hand that was once the one her father, Tebad, had brought in to be repaired. Pointing toward Kayla, Vandor asked, "Grandfather, why couldn't you fix that sword?"

Attentive, all sat to eat.

MaZak began with a chuckle, "Are you saying I am no good?"

Smiling, Vandor replied, "No grandfather. I just thought you could fix any sword."

"Sure, I could fix the sword if you mean to make it look pretty, but that doesn't mean it would be useful," explained MaZak.

"Take a book claiming to be fact, for instance. Each book has an author and publisher. If the author be unknown, how then can one trust the book? The cover may be nice to behold and the material may look of the highest quality, but can one truly know the honesty of the author or the validity of the publisher until it is read and handled? By then it could be too late; for what if one is taught a lie, most assuredly shall it be passed down and told until it possesses the same authority as truth.

"What then if it should fall apart even though the best care has been used, shall then the reader blame themselves or shall they acknowledge that though it looked the highest quality, it was but a counterfeit of lesser?

"So then is the sword. Whereas the publisher's name is viewed through the artwork and stability of the book, if he were to change the author's words without right, then the author's name would be slandered and his truth turned into a lie.

"As a swordsman, especially named among the *Sealed*, who claim to follow the *King*, I am expected to use only the purest material from the *King's* own stock. If I were to use a counterfeit piece of lesser quality, whether known or unknown by myself, if by chance my conscience would allow such, would I then remain worthy to be named among the *Sealed* or yet stay a friend to the *King*?

"What if I take one's sword, known by me to be of the poorest taste, shall I mix it with the pure to allow it to behold the luster of the real only to be frail and useless underneath? Shall I give it to such a one, when knowing that most assuredly it shall fail in battle, therefore sending one straight to death's door? Would I not be enabling the victory of the servants of *Darkness*, in as much as I fail to give the *King's* men whole heartedly what is proper and has been made especially for them?

"Dear children, to fix a sword as that which Kayla holds would be an injustice to the buyer, the maker, and the *King*. If one so desire for it to remain a relic, so be it, let it remain as it is. Yet, by chance, if one wish that it should be converted or renewed to assume the likeness of that of the *King's* proper, let it not be so among any swordsman.

"By such shall the buyer go away happy only to be sorrowed in battle.

Then assuredly shall the deed go forth unto all the villages as a testimony to the character of the one which formed it. Then shall the one which has done such mischief be placed upon center stage to answer the charges.

"Would not the buyer then assume that the *King* himself has sold the swordsman bad goods and is yet also to blame? Should then the swordsman take responsibility for his misconduct to exonerate the *King's* name, or shall he curse the *King* and free himself? Let it not be so among the *King's* men.

"So then shall I and every swordsman obey his conscience and the *King's Whisper* in using the pure stock of the *King* without the slightest idea of mixing it with that of lesser. Then shall the buyer be satisfied in battle, the conscience of the swordsman shall not be seared, and the name of the *King* left unblemished.

"As a publisher takes the words of the author and but puts them in a pretty cover, not daring to change the words, so then is the swordsman that takes the *King's* pure material and but designs it an outward look. In likeness the words of the author remain true even without a cover, so does the *King's* substance without design.

"The style, shine, and carvings upon the sword do not protect one in battle, but the underlying substance does hold or fail to one's gain or loss. Do not pick a sword for its looks, for its worth is in its substance. Even as a book's worth should be judge by its content, so then should a sword. Appearance just makes it easier to sell."

Their eyes never moved as they listened to MaZak speak of the art of sword making. The children pondered his words while glancing between him and the curled sword while he spoke. Not completely able to grasp all of that which he spoke, but the meaning could settle in their hearts to come forth another time.

Tindal had never really followed in his father's footsteps with a desire as such, but Vandor often tinkered around in his grandfather's shop with Kayla and Rayhold. Nowhere near ready to make his own sword, he one day would be. He dreamed of becoming one of the *Sealed* and being given a name such as his grandfather, *The Bladesman*.

"How is your lunch little V?" asked MaZak, breaking Vandor's daydreaming trance.

As for now, he would have to be satisfied in being known as "little V."

# Old Enough For a Gift

**M**aZak stood and walked over to one of the many cabinets in his shop as the children finished their lunch. Two rolls made of fresh bread each morning with a slice of ham betwixt the halves, a couple of carrots and a drink of fresh water really hit the spot. They knew very little of the candies and syrupy drinks of Trachten, the few treats those who visit the markets sometimes bring back.

"I have something here for you three. I believe you may be old enough," claimed MaZak facing the children, and then turning back toward the cabinet in his shop.

Opening the door, he bent over and reached to the bottom shelf to take hold of a wooden box, with King Salvare's insignia engraved into the top. Made of cherry wood, the box was long and deep with the imprint of a silver roaring lion head. He took the box and placed it on the table. Pulling a small set of keys from his pocket, he unlocked the silver latches on both ends of the front. Slowly he put his keys back into his pocket.

The three could no longer contain themselves; they ran to the sides of MaZak with inquisitive eyes, with bread crumbs sprinkled upon their clothes.

"What is it grandfather?" asked Vandor, as Kayla and Rayhold smiled with anticipation.

"Patience little V, patience shall get you further than impatience ever will and it shall indeed keep you from mistakes, which we all wish we had less of. Once the excitement is over it is lost forever; would you not like for it to linger but a few more moments?" questioned MaZak.

The inside of the box began to glitter, as the sun shone through the window into the crack of the opening, as MaZak lifted the lid. Slowly, as if toying with the three, he opened the box till the lid was laid completely open. Revealed were three shiny, silver daggers. MaZak smiled, beholding his work expressly for them and the children were speechless. In the eyes of MaZak, the moment was more than he had hoped, maybe even more meaningful for him than the three which it was for.

"My dear children, behold your daggers of *Truth*," smiled MaZak, still looking into the box.

Speechless they gazed upon magnificent works of art that shone so brightly, the eye could but squint to embrace the sight; each blade seven inches long with a squared hilt, ending at a roaring lion head. The detail was flawless and the luster incomparable. They could scarcely remember beholding such beauty. The blades looked as though they could split a hair and each was engraved with its bearers' initial. None said a word, but looked, wanting desperately to touch.

MaZak slowly handed Kayla her dagger engraved with a 'K' near the hilt. She took it with delight. Holding out both hands, as if waiting to be given a small, delicate animal, she watched it pass from his hands to hers. He handed her also a small fitted sheath for it, with a loop which could be fastened to a belt.

After Kayla, MaZak gave the second to Rayhold, as Rayhold's eyes gazed at the sparkle of the 'R' upon his blade. Staring at the shiny blade, Rayhold moved it left to right in small slicing motions. He also received a sheath as Kayla.

Next, MaZak took the final dagger from the box and placed it in Vandor's hand. Holding it with his left, Vandor ran his right pointer along the

'V' as he studied every detail his grandfather had worked into it. Taking also the sheath from his grandfather, Vandor noticed the *King's* insignia upon it.

"Dear children these are for you. They have been made from the *King's* own substance; iron for the blade, with leather strapped around the grip. I have engraved each to personalize them as such, but remember that is not what makes them do well in battle. I do not expect you to need them today, but I fear that such a time cometh.

"As we live, there are those who will need defending and those who need slaying by the sword. It is true that the *marked*[f] servants of *Darkness*, namely the *Gottlos*, are lost to the *Dragon's* grip, but remember grace and mercy toward the common man that is but blind and deaf to the forces around him. He wishes to enjoy the safety and blessings of the *King* yet desires not to serve him, and in doing so may inadvertently serve the other.

"Prepare yourselves for service to the *King*, with thy body, mind, and spirit. Learn his law, read his book, and obey that others may follow. Fear not if you should faulter in your honest service to the *King*, for he himself has said he will give grace and mercy to those who do not deserve it. So must ye."

---

[f] the symbol of the wicked one, upon the right hand or forehead of the servants of Darkness

# Turning Points in History

*M*aZak packed his things for the morrow. He would be going to the semiannual market in the Land of the *Seekers*. He had been told many high dignitaries and renowned men may be there in Trachten at this time. He had been many previous years, and knew he must bring his best quality of work this trip.

Tindal, who had most often followed his father to the markets, had shied away from doing so in the last many years, since the birth of Vandor. Vandor, now seventeen, so much wanted to go with his grandfather, but Tindal would not allow it this year, as it was his son's final year of schooling. Although Tindal taught most of his son's learning, Tindal was very much a disciplinarian and believed in following the letter of the law.

Because MaZak was older, he knew it wasn't wise to take such a trip alone, especially with all of the merchandise. There could be the possibility of meeting a thief along the way, not to mention needing help to set up the booth once there. So, MaZak's friend Dartego, a man slightly younger and smaller built than he, agreed to accompany MaZak to the market, as he had for many years since Tindal had ceased.

§　　§　　§　　§

MaZak and Dartego fathers' had fought and perished during the *Dark Ages*, whereby the self-proclaimed king Judarius had put into motion the smothering out of all knowledge of the true *King*. Judarius had been one of King Salvare's inner circle, a man to be looked up to and admired, or so was thought. He had fooled the council and most of Erde, as a thief and a traitor.

Legends have told that Judarius was possessed by the spirit of the *Dragon*; some hold it was his greed of riches, some claim it was his pride to rule over the land of Erde, still others believe he was persuaded by the false *seers*, namely *pales*<sup>f</sup>, of that day. From friend to betrayer, Judarius turned against King Salvare one night while the *King* walked among his garden.

King Salvare was taken by force that night while his men slept. He fought not against Judarius and his men as they came to take hold of him, calling Judarius "friend" till the end. To this day, no one knows how Judarius was able to sear his conscience to the point of turning against the *King* and all that is right.

Judarius rebuked the *King's* words of wisdom before all and told of his army of *Gottlos* and *Ubils* that would slay all those that would not serve him. Judarius claimed if Salvare was the true *King*, he could free himself. Judarius hung King Salvare upon a tree in open space to cause people to dread him by power. People cheered (because of panic, not joy) as Judarius' men moved among them causing fright, and demanding them to make their voices heard as if in excitement.

The people refrained from speaking out against Judarius. They were partially confused, because the people did believe the *King* was powerful enough to save himself, yet could not understand why he did not. Why a man as powerful as King Salvare would allow himself to be tortured and hung made no sense to the people. Where were his blessed *Sealed*? Where was his powerful father, Allmachtig, which dwelt in Himmel? Why did the *Sealed* not fight to free

---

<sup>f</sup> a male sorcerer, user of dark magic, false seer, which is most often deathly pale in color

their *King*? Surely, his father had been given word, why had he not sent his entire army to save his son from such death?

It was a sad day in the land of Erde, for even King Salvare's men, the very *Sealed*, held their peace, and most fled for fear of losing their own lives. From soldiers to cowards, overnight it seemed the common people, that were enticed by the words of King Salvare but never really followers of them, were confounded by the acts of the *Sealed*, the absence of his father, and were easily drawn into obedience to Judarius by the horror of his *Gottlos* and *Ubils*.

§     §     §     §

But victory of Judarius over King Salvare was short lived, or so was thought. King Allmachtig did get word, and did make himself known to the people of Erde, though they never saw him. By the power of King Salvare's father, King Allmachtig from the land of Himmel, King Salvare was made alive and appeared unto his servants, the *Sealed*, and many others in the land of Erde.

He spoke of mighty things to come and told them to scribe his words into the *Book of Wisdom* that the people may know the truth and beware of Judarius' delusions. He told them that he must depart unto the kingdom of his father for but a short while. King Salvare promised to return and destroy all that which was evil, and while away, his *Whisper* (an inward voice that speaketh the things of the *Book of Wisdom*, pricking the hearts of those who serve King Salvare) would remain. He promised to return with a new kingdom and to gather his people to a new dwelling he called New Erde.

§     §     §     §

Many called Judarius a devil. No one could recall the father of Judarius, and only his mother had claimed she was taken captive in the night and given child by one she could not see. She was as one that was possessed, a crazy woman; therefore, placed in solitude, where she perished alone. The *mark* was first seen upon her forehead, and thus was why she was given over to solitude away from the people. These things were not revealed till after Judarius betrayed King Salvare, for the *King* had wished to keep these things secret, so as to give Judarius an opportunity to work among the people without others continuously charging him with the sins of his father and mother.

Judarius was later slain by Balor, an infiltrator who claimed to be one of the last of the *Sealed*. Claims were made that Balor infiltrated through the ranks of Judarius' men, though never actually taking the *mark*. Some say he did take the *mark*, selling his soul to the *Darkness*, just to save Erde from Judarius' dark reign.

One may never know, for in the very night whereby he, along with a few of his trusted fellows, took Judarius out to be hung by his neck, Balor and his men were also slain, dismembered, and burned. Although the *Gottlos* were too late to save Judarius, they dared not let his murderers live.

At the death of Judarius, his lone heir Galtare took power and was enraged with hate! He burned all knowledge of King Salvare and his *Book of Wisdom* that he could attain. He killed men, women, and children alike who would not deny the *King* and swear allegiance to him. Being the son of a devil child, so called, the claim was made that Galtare being also the son of a devil, further meant all of his children forever were to be noted as the heirs of devils.

He destroyed villages only to leave the people desolate, so as to drive them into service by fear. Years of knowledge were lost and the land of Erde fell into dark times.

§　　§　　§　　§

But from the midst of fear arose men and women of might and courage, with understanding and truth. They found lost copies of King Salvare's *Book of Wisdom* and made haste to get them into the hands of the common people. They uncovered the mining of silver, gold, metals, and precious stones of the *King* and began to make themselves swords and weapons of war against the army of *Darkness*.

The children began to learn of the things which were once forbidden to speak of by Judarius and his son Galtare. It was the *Great Awakening* of beaten and torn lives, who had all but given up hope, which burst into a newness of life. New hope sprang forth from remembrance of King Salvare. Beacons of hope, a light in darkness, a new strength given to a hurting people, the *Sealed* were formed once more.

§ § § §

The final years of Galtare's life was spent mostly bedridden inside the castle upon Mount Dauthus, the mountain dead center of *Oscuridad*, for he had not strength enough to venture out. Some claimed he had gone out of his mind and thus it was why there was a decrease in violence and attacks. Others claimed he was merely preparing for another onslaught, which never came.

At the death of Galtare, who seemed to weaken and live sickly after slaying many people, his sons took charge over *Oscuridad*. To the eldest Jagare, he gave the central headship of *Oscuridad* on Mount Dauthus to rule over his ten brothers and their kingdoms. To the north of Mount Dauthus, in order from west to east, Galtare gave unto his sons Hatan, Baitrs, Gniew, Pyktis, and Zolba. To the south of Mount Dauthus in order from west to east, Galtare gave unto his sons Desgosto, Abejoti, Himo, Ahnews, and Begeren.

§ § § §

It had been less than a full generation since the *Great Awakening*, and already the people had grown content with their simple lives and easily dismissed the destruction of the smaller villages by servants of *Darkness*. With no sign of Jagare, many did not seem to notice or care that the *Gottlos* and *Ubils* still lived, as long as it did not hinder their lives. Selfish contentment moved people to consider only themselves, and if they were untouched by the servants of *Darkness*, they did nothing for those that were, lest the *Darkness* move upon them also.

When notices arrived of another village or group of people having been taken captive or murdered, blame was often placed upon the victims themselves, as if to say they could have avoided it by doing thus and such. Some even held the notion that if one were to leave the evil ones alone, not even speaking of such, then it would bear reason that they would do the same.

This type of thinking often seemed to fail to change, lest they themselves be taken over by the *Darkness*, and then their own cries heard as the ones they refused to give ear to. Who then is left to comfort those, who had no comfort for their brothers and sisters?

With such a mindset, it was left to the *Sealed*, the soldiers and *seers*, along with bands, which fought neither for King Salvare or Jagare, but self, namely militias and the *Masonisti*; to defend those which were prey for the servants of *Darkness*.

§ § § §

The *Sealed* lessened in number in recent years for there were those which said, "The *King* is not returning, but has forgotten us," "The *King* has left us to the mercy of Jagare and his brothers," and most gravely said, "It has been too long. King Salvare is but dead."

There was nearly never a mention of his father King Allmachtig from the lips of the people of Erde either. It had come to almost an *each man for himself* attitude of sorts.

Even the *Book of Wisdom* was seldom read or found being taught in school but for history's sake. Neither did the parents teach their children of such. They had become nothing more than simple history to some, only folklore to many, and merely lie to others.

Though there may have been a *Great Awakening*, there were many which remained in *Darkness*, and those who failed to embrace the truth or give service to the *King*.

# A Glance into Darkness

S tanding upon the highest mountain in *Oscuridad*, Mount Dauthus, laid Jagare's castle over his kingdom. It was a dark massive castle with ten foot stone walls and five-foot barbed fence layered atop them. No way in or out except through the main gates, which must only be opened at the sound of Jagare himself.

His kingdom was surrounded by six mountains and ten lesser kingdoms. Three mountains to either side and his brothers' five kingdoms to his north and five kingdoms to his south, Jagare was secure almost dead center of *Oscuridad*.

It was the *Shadow Lands* which separated *Oscuridad* from Trachten and the rest of Erde. A continuous haze from the *Shadow Lands* stagnated throughout *Oscuridad*, leaving Jagare's castle foggy, humid, and hot; most uncomfortable with no real water supply, but the bitter taste of the Kartus Ocean of which the moat surrounding Mount Dauthus flowed. Not that it bothered a man that had survived death himself.

§　　§　　§　　§

Legend had it that one of the *Sealed* had caught Jagare unaware in the land of Trachten, when he and his army were marching toward Signum, soon after the death of Galtare. A silver arrow from amidst the open plains pierced Jagare's head above his right temple. His servants rushed his body back to *Oscuridad*, but the people knew for sure he must have perished there. There was so much blood and confusion, yet the bowman was never found.

Many assumed it must have been one of the *Masonisti*, and therefore the reason why none had claimed the honor for themselves. Others considered the soul, who had been brave enough to pierce Jagare with an arrow, remained silent due to the fear of his life or the life of his family.

Following legend told that one named Piradad, a *pale*, appeared to the servants of Jagare within the castle walls without entrance through the gates. It was said that he was brought by a *Dragon* named *Rubicund* from Kriminala Pasaule, a land far south from the land of Erde. It was said that Piradad held powers from the underworld, given him by the *Dragon*.

Supposing it to be true, Piradad laid hands on Jagare with power from the *Dragon* and Jagare was healed, awakening from death. As with his grandfather Judarius, there were those that swore it was but the body of Jagare possessed by the *Dragon* himself. The son of a devil, from the lineage of devils, raised by the power of the *Dragon* by a *pale*, could only mean Jagare was now twofold the evil he once was.

§     §     §     §

Sitting in a room constructed of dark marble dimly lit, a man of graying age held the role of the king of *Darkness*, so named by those who opposed him. The room was large and hollow. Windows with dark stained glass every twenty paces were the only breaks besides the entrance around the square walls. To the norm it would seem cold and dry, with the smell of staleness lingering in every molecule of air.

Dressed in dark attire, as if a shadow amidst the throne, slightly leaning to one side upon his elbow, he played with his large golden ring engraved with a dragon's head. Thoughts of mischief and malice ran sadistically through his depraved mind as he pondered what was, what now is, and what would come.

"Piradad, come forth," he growled deeply.

"Yes, master Jagare," claimed one as he stepped up to the throne with a bow. Dressed to much the same likeness as a *seer* of the *Sealed*, he wore a black cloak (whereas theirs are mostly brown, white, or tan), and carried a staff which often left one to ponder *does it hold any significance or purpose as to the role of seer.*

Nails, as talons, protruded from his boney, pale fingers, gripping his smoked colored staff. It glimmered lightly by the few lit candles, as though it were covered with a shiny glaze. His hand bore the *mark*, the seal of sworn allegiance, by which once taken, the bearer's soul was bound by contract to the king of *Darkness*.

"What seest thou?" asked Jagare in a defiant voice.

In a deep, guttural accent, Piradad answered, "My lord, I have seen the destruction of the *Sealed*. The infiltration has been most successful, and the spies await your sign. Among the cities of the lands, there are those which silently serve you and shall raise up against your enemies at the sound of your voice, my lord. Your patience shall pay off King Jagare, for it has caused the people to grow confident and slack that you shall not attack."

"Send for the *Gibborims* of the ten kingdoms (by this he meant his brothers). Have them come to Mount Dauthus on the night of the next full moon. The time approaches for all men everywhere to bow to their master! The hour cometh when the *Dragon* shall slay the people of the dead *King* which doth deny us our rightful place."

"Yes, my lord," answered Piradad.

"Have the engravers finished the image?" snapped Jagare.

"Yes, my lord, they are awaiting your command," Piradad answered again, stronger this time.

As if irritated for the mere fact of having to ask the question at all, Jagare sneered, "Have the *Gottlos* and *Ubils* been counted?"

"Yes, my lord," Piradad replied with confidence.

Jagare continued angrily, "Send one third to Trachten. Inform them that one is to live for testimony only."

"Yes, my lord," Piradad replied again, knowing from experience this was the best response to keep one from the rebuke of Jagare.

Jagare waved Piradad away. As Piradad left the room, Jagare rubbed the side of his head where there was only the faint hint of a small scar upon his temple, but a reminder nevertheless. Though he knew not the name of the soul who pierced him, all of Erde would suffer his wrath for it.

# A Goodbye to Remember

*T*he sunrise was beautiful. Slowly, a spotlight rose in the sky with shades of purple, yellow, and red flowing from it. Peeking over the mountains and large oaks and sycamores, it gave a marvelous display of radiance. Sparkling through the puffy clouds with colors of white and blue, a new day dawned. A soft, crisp breeze delivered the scent of fresh flowers accompanied by calmness among the village.

MaZak and Dartego were making last minute checks, to ensure they had packed all they would need for the journey to the Land of the *Seekers*, when Vandor walked up behind them. Wishing very much he could accompany them had robbed him of countless hours of sleep the last few nights.

"Good morning," greeted Vandor with a small grin.

MaZak turned around to focus on the voice behind him, "Hey there, little V."

"Good morning young Vandor," added Dartego as he faced his direction.

"Today is a beautiful day," commented MaZak.

"Yes MaZak, the sun will shine on us today and the breeze should lend us traveling ease," agreed Dartego.

"I agree Dartego," MaZak replied while gazing upward.

All three stared intently at the sky in a moment of silence.

MaZak reached to place his hand atop Vandor's shoulder, "Come little V, I have something for you over here." Vandor's eyes widened and his heart sped a little. Leaving Dartego by the horses and wagon, they walked over to MaZak's shop.

The building held the look of weathered-treated wood, yet sturdy, with a large painted sign over the entrance that read 'Metal Works' in bold black writing. All the shutters to the windows had been lowered and locked to keep out scavengers while he would be away. They walked through the entrance which was still open from gathering last minute supplies.

"Vandor you will soon be a man...If not one already," MaZak exclaimed with a small chuckle, while facing the same cabinet from which he had once pulled forth three daggers. From the bottom shelf as before, MaZak reached for the wooden box with King Salvare's insignia. Vandor could only imagine what surprise the box held for him this time, for the dagger was more than he could ever imagine. Still worn on his hip, he subconsciously felt the pommel lion head of the dagger with his fingertips.

MaZak removed the locks on the box and lifted back the lid to reveal something wrapped in an old grey frayed cloth. Vandor stood still with school boy excitement. MaZak removed the item and placed it on the wooden bench where he did his engraving work. Taking his time as before to embrace the moment, he slowly laid back the folded cloth one layer at a time, and Vandor dared not say a word to break the silence.

The last fold of cloth was moved to reveal a masterpiece of the finest craftsmanship. Vandor waited to see what was revealed: a shine that was blinding with the engraving of a 'V', which extended the length of the sword on both sides; a solid squared hilt wrapped with light brown leather; a double-edged blade sharp enough to cut frog hair and flowing to a tip that could pin a tick to the ground; a guard strait across and a pommel, as the dagger, in the shape of a silver roaring lion. Accompanied by a leather sheath with King Salvare's silver insignia close to the top, these were truly works of art. Vandor was well pleased.

MaZak turned his head to see Vandor staring with his mouth open. "Do you like it?" he asked.

"Grandfather…You…This is the finest sword my eyes have ever seen. When did you find such time to form it?" Vandor questioned excitedly.

"Many late nights little V, many late nights," MaZak answered.

"I am forever grateful. I shall wear it with pride," stammered Vandor.

"I assume you like it then," smiled MaZak.

"More so, grandfather. It is the greatest gift I have ever been given. Even more so than my beloved dagger," Vandor grinned with enthusiasm.

"Vandor, use it wisely. I have trained you somewhat over the years, but there is much for you to learn. We shall recover the thought at my return. A fine soldier of the *King* you may become." MaZak paused to take a breath, looking down then returning his eyes to Vandor, "Do you believe the *Book of Wisdom* from the *King*, little V?"

"Yes grandfather, I have no reason to doubt you," Vandor replied.

"I do not ask if you believe me Vandor, but do you believe that which is written?" MaZak pressed.

"Yes grandfather, I believe it all to be true," Vandor assured him.

MaZak displayed a sign of relief, or was it satisfaction; it was too quick to tell.

"Vandor, if you believe the Book then you must believe the *King*. Though you cannot see him, you must believe that he is. This sword is made with the *King's* pure stock; it is rightfully from him to you to do his service. You will never be able to wear the *King's* armor and be protected in battle against those who shall rise up against him and his people if you do not trust him."

MaZak continued, "You must defend the *King's* teachings against those who oppose it, tell others of King Salvare, and do your best to protect them from the servants of *Darkness*. Even today there are those who know nothing of King Salvare or consider him but folklore."

"Grandfather, you have often spoken of these things. Why do you speak as though you are upon your bed to fall asleep forever? Shall you not return from Trachten in a couple of weeks? Thou knowest I believe and will be glad to converse with you upon your return. I most wish I could accompany you to the markets this year. If only father would allow me such pleasure," Vandor pleaded.

"I fear that by my apprehension of too much study I have neglected needed surety of your knowledge of the *Book of Wisdom*, replacing it with an over abundance of battle techniques with the sword," MaZak pondered. "There must be a balance."

"Do you mean like father, always study and law?" Vandor questioned.

"Um..." a breath, as he felt the *Whisper* move within him, "knowing the art of battle without belief in the *Book of Wisdom* leaves one fighting for what? To fulfill a thirst of blood? No, Vandor. To know the *Book of Wisdom* is to know the cause of why we stand and trust the *King*, giving reason as to why we follow. We do not fight for the love of fighting; we defend the *King* and his words from the *Darkness* to keep those whom the *Darkness* would love to catch unaware and consume."

MaZak paused as if to clear his thoughts, "I cannot be with you always little V. You must take what you have been taught and use it wisely. You must desire that which is right; against youthful lusts and foolish thoughts you must persist.

"Do not allow yourself to be caught up in the pleasures of this world to lose sight of your duties and the return of King Salvare. Do not let him return to see you wasting away in a life of lasciviousness, dishonesty, and mischief. Hold strong to your faith in the *King* and his words and let not those which despise him cause you to waver. Though you cannot see him, be still, and hear King Salvare's *Whisper* speak within you from the words in his Book."

Vandor pondered these things in his heart as his grandfather spoke. He felt sure his grandfather knew he much believed the Book of the *King* and long desired to see him and the *Shimmering* kingdom. *Why does he speak as though he does not know such and as if he will not return?* Vandor wanted to ask, but his thoughts were broken by his grandfather handing him yet something else.

MaZak pulled his hand again from the box, pulling out a dark brown pouch with a white leather tie. "Give Kayla these. She asked me sometime last week if I would find time to make her some."

Vandor searched the pouch, "How many arrow heads did you make her grandfather?"

"There are probably thirty in there, but tell her I can make more when she needs them," MaZak replied.

"Yes grandfather. She certainly favors the bow."


Locking up the shop, they returned to Dartego who was propped up snoozing against the rear wheel of the wagon. "Wake up lazy soldier," shouted MaZak.

"I hear yah, grandfather," laughed Dartego as he opened his eyes.

"Little V, did you hear what this worn out boot-warmer said?" chuckled back MaZak.

Dartego picked up a stick, "Well, I've got your staff here in case one of your bowed legs give out."

The two carried on for a few minutes while Vandor stood by sheepishly grinning, hoping he would not be so silly at that age.


They said their goodbyes and made one last glance around to ensure all was secure in the wagon. Hugs were exchanged.

"When I return I shall no longer call you little V," said MaZak. "Yc shall no longer be little, but a man."

"I shall await your return then," answered Vandor with a grin. Vandor lifted his hand in the air as he watched them travel out of sight.

# Joys for the Moment

*V*andor, holding a ring on his pointer, rounded the corner and saw Kayla sitting among the flowers behind her home near the edge of the east of Nesal, as she often did. It was a pricey silver ring; perfectly shaped with '*Kayla*' inscribed around it, with a small daisy on each side of her name. Vandor had also inscribed '*love Vandor*' upon the inner circle. It took him little more than a week to consider it perfect, spending hours on each little detail.

For the moment he just watched her. The sunlight glistened through her auburn hair as it waved at him in the breeze. The fragrance of sweet perfume gave his heart delight. Was it the smell of the flowers or Kayla which awakened his senses, he could not tell. His heart pressed to move him forward, but his mind held his feet secure to the ground.

Sitting in a field of flora, Kayla sang to herself a song that many mothers shared with their children to ease their little minds at night. Her voice was beautiful to him. She was beautiful to him. He wished to tell her of his love, but was afraid to risk such friendship to be left with nothing.

What if she does not love him back, could he yet face her on the morrow? No. They must remain friends; he must deny himself the pleasure of revealing his heart. Taking a moment to examine the ring, *Oh how much I wish to tell thee*, he thought and placed it back into his pocket.

Vandor removed his sword from the sheath, as he held the pouch of arrow heads with his other hand. Slowly he moved toward Kayla, careful not to break as much as a twig.

The closer he found himself, the more his heart began to patter. Subconsciously grinning from ear to ear, almost unable to keep himself from running, he forced himself to hold pace. She seemed most unaware of his approach, singing and picking flowers while holding them close to her nose. Vandor was upon her –

She twisted in swift motion raising her dagger toward his chest! "Beg for mercy *Gottlo*," she cried.

It was Vandor who was taken by surprise, dropping his sword and falling backwards to the ground. She softly smiled and Vandor felt the warmth of embarrassment overcome his cheeks.

"The flowers are marvelous this time of year," she claimed while still holding the daisy and dagger. "They hold a much fresher smell than that of *Gottlos* who try to sneak up upon fair maidens unaware." Smiling, "Wouldn't you say, dear Vandor?"

"Huh," Vandor replied, for completely reversed the joke had become.

"Oh, do come V and sit with me a while," Kayla said as she turned her back to him, and placed the dagger near her side.

Somewhat disgusted that he failed to surprise her and a little humbled by how she had turned the tables, he moved near her, but not too close. "How then were you able to sense me," he wondered.

"The flowers gave you away dear Vandor," she slyly replied.

"Shall I slay them for tattling then?" he asked.

"Spare them, for they are but children," she answered.

"Shall I grant them mercy then, only to be spoiled again another day?" Vandor asked merely going along, for Kayla often enjoyed this type of play.

"For my sake I ask it," Kayla pleaded.

"Then let it be as ye ask," Vandor conceded.

Changing thought, Vandor stated, "I have brought you a gift from my grandfather."

She looked up from the flowers, "For me? What type of gift?"

"Ah, it will cost you a fair price," Vandor grinned.

"I have neither silver nor gold," she admitted.

"It will cost you but a question," said Vandor, eager to know how she knew he was there.

"Fair enough. Ask away dear Vandor," she approved.

"I was careful not to break so much as a twig. How is it that you knew I was behind you," Vandor begged.

"Your shadow did betray you, as the sun cast it over my shoulder," Kayla smiled and looked at him with sparkling eyes.

Answered, Vandor could do nothing but relinquish the prize.

Kayla laid down the daisy, which was missing a few petals, to look inside the pouch. She pulled out an arrow head to examine it, "These are very well made Vandor. Your grandfather always does such good work. He needn't have made me so many."

"He said that if you should ever need more, be sure to tell him," Vandor explained.

"I am very grateful Vandor. I shall make sure to tell him such at his return to Nesal," she gleefully responded.

"He will be delighted to know that," he acknowledged.

Seeing the flicker of light against his new blade, Kayla asked, "Vandor, is that new?" while she pointed to his sword.

"Yes, grandfather gave it to me before his departure to Trachten this morning, as with this sheath and your arrow heads."

She reached out, "May I see it?"

Vandor was delighted she asked and was proud to let her hold it.

"This is a most fabulous creation V, maybe even his best work," Kayla declared with eyes wide open, examining every inch of the blade, moving it left and right by turning her wrist.

"I did tell him as much when he gave it," agreed Vandor.

Shifting her eyes from the sword to Vandor she asked, "What of you Vandor? Have you also brought me a gift?"

Wanting to say yes, but already in an uncomfortable moment, as he had intended to give her the ring yet had chosen otherwise, he smartly said, "Is my presence not enough?"

She grinned, "Indeed Vandor, I very much appreciate your presence."

Delighted and shocked, expecting a sly remark he felt his cheeks redden a little, "And I yours' Kayla."

"Vandor, what shall we do in coming years," she asked intently looking down at the daisy she once held missing the petals.

"What do you mean Kayla?"

"I mean we have been friends forever it seems. Do you think life will lead us down different paths?" she questioned, again as she faced him.

The conversation had turned more serious and Vandor felt somewhat awkward, "I..." His mind was full of things to say and ponder, but could he share them? "I hope not Kayla."

Silenced for a moment, "Why Vandor?" she asked intently as if trying to pry something from his very heart.

He felt scared and unsure of what to say, "What would I do without you and Rayhold to pal with?"

Her eyes looked downward as if somewhat disappointed, "Yes, we are a fancy trio, aren't we?"

Vandor tried to shift the conversation, "I would like to be named among the *Sealed*, to be one of the *King's* army."

Her eyes again looked upward, plucking another petal from the daisy,

"I myself have thought as much."

"While growing up, we have always said that would be our dream. To join the *Sealed* and fight the army of *Darkness*," Vandor explained.

"Yes Vandor," she replied, "but sometimes things we say as children are simply childish things that have no meaning."

Somewhat confused, not knowing what she meant, he asked, "What do you mean Kayla?"

She looked at him with her gentle green eyes. He was drawn in by her delicate face and the glow of sunlight through her auburn hair. He watched her soft lips as if in slow motion, "You once told me that you loved me when we were younger, Vandor."

A breath as she pulled the last petal from the daisy she held, "Do you feel as such for me now that we are older?"

His palms began to sweat, as his mind was too garbled to speak. Was this not what he wanted to know himself? Did she feel the same for him, or had he just been too obvious? Was there a right or wrong answer? Was this the right time, the only time? What if he just let it pass by, would there be a tomorrow that was better?

"I..." He reached into his pocket, looking toward his hand and pulled out the ring. For a moment he looked at it, and then extended his hand to Kayla. "I made this for you."

Dropping the stem she was holding, she noticed the daisies on both sides of her name as it set in Vandor's palm. She slowly reached to pick it up. She saw *'love Vandor'* in the center circle, and lifted her eyes to him again, "Do you love me Vandor?"

Her voice was so soft, her look so beautiful and honest.

Vandor stared into her eyes, knowing it was now or never, "I do Kayla. I have always loved you."

The pressures of his heart seemed to release, giving way to a freedom he had longed for.

"I have forever waited for this moment. From since you had first told me as children, I have desired so to hear it again," she gasped, "I too love you Vandor."

The fear is gone, replaced with relief and excitement which words could not express. Even hearing her say the words was like a dream he would awaken from at any moment.

"I was afraid that you did not feel the same," he confessed.

"And I thought it was only a childish crush you had all but forgotten," she admitted.

"I often desired to tell you, but fear did move me from saying so."

Kayla slid the ring on her finger, "I accept your love Vandor and freely give you my heart in return," she said with excitement.

Their hearts nervously pattered. Eyes met and they slightly bowed toward one another. A pause as the sunlight glowed between their facial silhouettes closed in. Their eyes closed as they felt the warmth of the other's breath upon their skin. A soft moist press of the lips, long awaited, it was a most cherished moment by both. Little more than a peck, but smiles covered their faces. Freshness filled the air that overshadowed the smell of the flowers. It must be love. It was in their tear-filled eyes. *I love you...*

# Desire for the Supernatural

ayhold saw Vandor kiss Kayla among the flowers, as he slipped into the oaks and sycamores around the village. He had been looking for them, but now did not seem to be the time.

It was no secret to him that these two had a fondness for one another, but it did seem to hinder their friendship somewhat, with Vandor and Kayla spending more time together, leaving him feeling somewhat unwanted and left out. They never discouraged his fellowship, nor appeared to want him to leave, but he began to feel like a fifth leg to a wart hog; simply just in the way. *It's not really jealousy* he told himself, *it's just how life goes.*

For some time, maybe six months or more, Rayhold had secretly been meeting with a young man by the name of Onyx. A dark fellow, though not skin mind you, for he was quite white. Not the Caucasian white, nor the albino, more the type that never saw the sun. He was a *pale*, with grey eyes, wearing a hooded black cloak, which seemed to glide from place to place without being noticed.

Peculiar indeed, but most inquisitive was Rayhold about him and his abilities, shall we say. Rayhold knew very well it was against the law, but ever since their first encounter he craved to learn more. More of the so called talents, this Onyx claimed all men had, but few there be which dug into the depth of themselves to allow such forces of power to flow forth from them.

§    §    §    §

On the night of the full moon, sometime last fall, Rayhold was near the edge of the village, practicing with his dagger from MaZak, upon a rotten oak stump, when Onyx startled him from behind. Rayhold felt uneasy at first, with a sudden sense of chill in the air. Though slightly uncomfortable, there was an enticement about Onyx which held Rayhold there.

*Is this a servant of Darkness or a danger to the village*, he thought. He did not know, for it was no doubt a stranger he had never seen. He stood motionless wanting to draw first, already being caught off guard. Unsure of who and what, seconds seemed like minutes. Odd, he felt scared, though not, at the same time.

"My dear Rayhold, fear not, I have not come to harm thee," claimed the figure.

Rayhold was still tense, gripping his dagger somewhat tighter. Hundreds of thoughts passed through his mind, yet none carried with them any coherency.

"I have come to give thee knowledge beyond thy wildest dreams," the stranger continued with a low voice. "Thou hast been handpicked to be given special insight over thy peers, shall thou choose to accept it, of course. Thou already possess the ability, one must only reach out to it and take hold."

With a little strength, Rayhold responded, "Who are you?"

"Indeed my name," answered the visitor, "You may call me Onyx."

"Why me?" questioned Rayhold, with a tremble in his voice.

"You have been chosen," Onyx returned.

"Chosen…What do you mean chosen? Who chose me," Rayhold still questioned.

"You ask many questions, but do you seek the answers," calmly said

Onyx.

"What...what do you mean?" Rayhold replied.

"I mean, do thou ask because ye do not know, or do ye ask because ye want to know?" Onyx questioned Rayhold.

Rayhold felt slightly confused, "I...I don't understand why someone would be looking for me."

"Are we not all looking for something? Dear Vandor has found love in young Kayla. Kayla has found dreams to come true with Vandor. Yet they trust not one another to share those feelings as of yet," whispered Onyx.

"Where are thy dreams young Rayhold, and who is it that thou doest have? Do ye not desire to be among the mighty men, among the renowned figures of old? Do ye not ponder the thoughts of prominence among mortals, to be esteemed highly in the eyes of all?" continued Onyx.

Rayhold wondered, *how does he know of such.* "I don't even know you. How can I trust you?"

Onyx replied, "How then may I trust ye, if thou do not trust me," leaving Rayhold with only more questions circling around in his mind.

Onyx lifted his arm parallel to the ground palm upwards. "Take thy dagger and cut my hand, young Rayhold."

Surprised Rayhold replied beginning to lean backwards, "What...Why would I cut your hand?"

"So that we may trust one another," Onyx gave response.

"How will cutting you build trust? How do I know you will not cut me next?" questioned Rayhold.

"As thou hast said, ye do not know, for this we must trust. I must trust that ye will do as I ask, and thou must trust I will do as I have said. Cut me, for I shall not touch thee, I mean only to give thou a glimpse of what thou mayest want," demanded Onyx slightly changing his tone.

Rayhold eyed his dagger, but confusion still controlled his thoughts for the moment. *This makes no sense. Cut me so we can trust each other. But what does he want to show me? If I don't cut him I won't find out, but if I do, what then if he wishes to slay me? What if this is a trick and I am told to my parents or the village? Surely they will be scared of me and call me a lunatic or worse. What if it is true and he has something interesting to show me? Vandor and Kayla have each other. Maybe I could pretend to follow him just to learn what he wants to show me. I could always run and tell people he tried to grab me and took my dagger. Surely Vandor and Kayla would believe me, along with MaZak.*

"Do ye wish to know that which I have come to show thee or not young Rayhold," Onyx called with a bit of exasperation in his tone. "Cut me boy, that I may know thou art worthy of such teachings!"

Rayhold jumped, and walked slowly over to the hooded man.

Most awkward he felt but he could not overcome the curiousness in what this foreigner may actually have known that he didn't. Rayhold's palm sweated as he held the dagger as tight as he could. The thought of running was still in his mind, the closer he got to the stranger the more he desired to know exactly what Onyx intended to do after he cut him.

Standing within a foot of one another, Onyx's deep voice said, "Cut me Rayhold. Fear not, thou will not hurt me. Trust my voice and heed to what it says."

Rayhold slowly lifted the blade of the dagger over Onyx's palm. Rayhold's arm moved the blade, as if by its self, splitting and folding the flesh back as it slid across the bare skin of Onyx. Blood flowed from the wound and dripped to the green grass below.

Rayhold was amazed as Onyx had not twitched the slightest. He held the dagger still in the air, fixated on Onyx's palm not really knowing what to expect next. Blood still dripped from the blade to the ground.

Onyx's palm began to heal itself. As the skin sealed, the blood returned to its veins. Rayhold blinked; multiple times he blinked. *This must be a trick.* But the stranger had not moved his hand and Rayhold had been watching. He knew for sure that his blade had cut Onyx, for blood was still yet upon it and drops remained on the grass.

*Is it a miracle? Is this what he wants to teach me? What a grand idea!* Rayhold considered.

"Do thou now wish to learn that which I present?" Onyx posed.

"I..." a pause for thought, "But, sorcery is against the law," Rayhold insisted.

"Only for the sake of control does it remain. The law is old and the writers are dead. So let their foolish words vanish with them. Embrace the power Rayhold and become a god among men," Onyx taunted.

"But if found out, they will wish to slay me or worse, burn me at the stake as a witch or law breaker," Rayhold begged.

"Dear Rayhold, have ye learned nothing? Did thou not see my hand yet heal the wound ye imposed? Follow me and I shall show thee how to cheat death itself," offered Onyx.

So began the relationship of Rayhold and Onyx as Rayhold slipped into the desires of sorcery. Vandor and Kayla seldom noticed Rayhold not being around, not that they did not still care for him, but their minds were fixed upon each other.

§　　　§　　　§　　　§

Stepping deep into the oaks and sycamores, Rayhold set down on a tree stump that appeared to have been there for quite some time. (Still solid, the stump allowed him to rest his weight, slouching somewhat and looking at the ground.)

After seeing Vandor and Kayla, he recalled there was a girl that he saw once in Qualtes just south of Nesal, named Cenobia, who caught his eye. Her skin was a shade darker than his, with large dark brown eyes, and full lips under her slightly pudgy nose. She looked simple, not outlandishly beautiful, but appealing to the eye in a most natural way to him. As if he saw who and how she was, not simply her outward appearance.

He knew only minimal about her, for they had only spoken to each other a few times over the past months, but she did stare and smile at him often though.

Maybe he could see if Vandor and Kayla would like to visit there tomorrow. There was clearly no one in Nesal that caught his eye.


From behind a tree appeared Onyx. "Dear Rayhold, what do ye sit there pondering?"

"Oh nothing," replied Rayhold.

"Dear Rayhold, why do thou yet lie to me? Have I not given thee that which thou desire," asked Onyx.

"Forgive me. It is but a selfish thing," Rayhold looked down.

"Tell me then young Rayhold. Maybe I could help."

Rayhold looked to Onyx, *of course he can*. "There is a girl in Qualtes that I would much like to see again."

"Thou speak of young Cenobia," Onyx answered, "and indeed I may be able to help."

"How…how do you know that," Rayhold exclaimed.

"I know many things," laughed Onyx.


Onyx pulled an amulet from his pocket. It was white with faint swirls of gray running throughout. In the shape of a rose bloom two inches in size, it was attached to a black twine necklace through one of the petals.

Onyx grinned, holding the rose and allowing the twine to dangle, "Place this around her neck. She will love thee for it."

Rayhold smiled, holding out his hand to take it, "This is nice. Where did you get it?"

"I've had it for quite some time. Take it. It will do what thou please," Onyx handed it over, ensuring Rayhold of its power.

Rayhold held the rose in his palm examining the detail; the craftsmanship was of high quality. *This is beautiful.*

"Yes Rayhold, it is," Onyx replied to his thoughts aloud.

Rayhold looked up, "You've got to teach me that."

"Not all at once young Rayhold. Patience and practice," Onyx explained. "Shall we being then?"

# Trachten,

# The Land of the Seekers

*T*rachten was an extremely large area in the land of Erde. The land was mostly desert with little vegetation. If it weren't for the Umeten Canal, which ran near the top of the city, there would have been no Trachten. While the canal was being dug, members had to haul in water from the Liban River, which fed the canal. The size of the city would never have survived had this still been necessary. They took whatever they wanted from the river through the canal, allowing the rest to continue on.

Hence the name the Land of the *Seekers* has been used as far back as any can remember. In the days before the canal, those seeking to escape the *Shadow Lands* would often die before they could reach the Liban River to the east. For that reason most would dare not try to leave and often were snatched into the *Darkness* of *Oscuridad*. Instead of trying to escape, they simply accepted their fate. The small stretch of *Shadow Lands* was all that separated Trachten from *Oscuridad*, and was full of many unspeakable pleasures of this world.

When the *Sealed* first helped build the canal, many people came from the west being led out of the *Shadow Lands* across the desert, now known as Trachten, but the numbers crossing over slowed drastically. Those from the *Shadow Lands* began only to go as far as Trachten to wander amidst the semiannual markets, but no further. They found all they needed in the Land of the *Seekers*, and returned to the *Shadow Lands* with their desires being filled. They no longer feared the *Darkness*, as Jagare had seemingly been silent these past years.

Xima was the name of the governor of Trachten, whose family broke ground and dug the Umeten Canal, accepting help from the *Sealed*. The city received its name from its originator, Sir Trachten, grandfather in the lineage of Xima. He was a very wealthy, intelligent man.

Legend had it that Sir Trachten somewhat disliked the laws of King Allmachtig, neither did he much care for the teachings of King Salvare, but he also feared the *Shadow Lands* and *Oscuridad*. For this cause he took all that he had, which was much, and settled in the desert away from all.

Since that day, Sir Trachten's generations have remained there, especially since the idea of a semiannual market, which saw thousands upon thousands of people from all over, bringing in mighty fine revenue indeed. They remained a family of wealth, claiming never to pledge their allegiance either to the *King* or the *Darkness*. The Trachten generations proclaimed neutrality, gladly accepting any and all benefits from both those of the *King* and those of the *Darkness*.

§     §     §     §

MaZak and Dartego traveled for days and finally arrived in Trachten. It was a long trip, stopping only in Goslet for a night and Salong for another; they were more than ready to rest a while. The closer they got to Trachten, the dryer the climate became, the hotter the days, and the colder the nights. They already missed the fresh mountain air of Nesal.

Entering Trachten, they still had to travel somewhat a distance to Palvolin where the markets were actually held. Due south of Telbaton, central Trachten, furthest from the Umeten Canal, it was dry and dusty, but had the most room for all the people. It was also far from the palace of Xima and the majestic parts of Trachten in Xiacon where the prominent lived. Originally near the center of Trachten, in Telbaton, the markets had hence moved to Palvolin, more south west, in the last ten years.

They stopped at the same place they always did, to pay for a room for the week. Most of the dignitaries and renowned fellows stayed north a good ways at Yoto's Inn. Near Xima's palace, it was fancier and higher priced than at Brocolat's. Yoto's had maids that tended to washing, meals, and what not, whereas Brocolat's was merely do-it-yourself rooms.

Whereas Brocolat's surroundings were simple and bland, Yoto's Inn, being closer to the palace in Xiacon, laid also among the less godly establishments of Trachten, which the *Sealed* had taken oath to refrain from.

The time of these markets were an occasion to reacquaint friendships, sell ones goods (whereas they may had trouble doing if limited to only their own villages), to peer into the talents and merchandise of others, but also for many wealthy souls, it was a time for indulgency of their lusts.

"I don't know about you good friend, but I think I'm getting somewhat old," claimed MaZak, bringing the wagon to a halt.

"Aye, you look pretty old," Dartego replied smiling.

MaZak returned a chuckle.

MaZak and Dartego stepped up to the old wooden counter. Full of chips and splinters with scribbling here and there carved into the surface, it hadn't been replaced in a while. The smell of sawdust on the floors brought back memories every year. Around the way came the attendant. The total of four weeks a year for these markets was where Brocolat's made most of its money. It wasn't much to look at, but the owner and his workers had always seemed to be cheery, honest fellows.

"Hey Key," a nickname for obvious reasons, MaZak called out.

"MaZak and Dartego," noted Key "We missed you last trip around here Dartego."

"Yeah, I wasn't able to make it the last trip," Dartego replied.

"What about you MaZak? Got anything fancy this trip?" asked Key.

"I may have something you like," MaZak claimed with a smile, "but you'll have to wait till the morrow. We need some rest."

"Park your wagon behind the place and you can put your horses in the stables. This will give you more protection," explained Key.

"Been having problems lately?" asked Dartego.

"I just don't want anything coming up missing and you two blaming me. Last trip a guy blamed me for his trinkets coming up missing. Said his wagon was parked out front, so it was my fault. Made a big stink, but turns out he was just lying, so we ran him out of town."

"I see. You take the guy's stuff, and then run him out of town," MaZak smiled.

"Sounds like that's what happened to me," added Dartego.

"Ah, I can see now this is going to be a long week with you two," grinned Key.

§    §    §    §

Morning came early, but MaZak and Dartego were ready to greet it. Cricket's Eatery was the small tavern next door to the inn, where most eating was done on makeshift wooden benches and tables outside around the front and back. One had to make sure not to get a splinter or two. As they didn't serve wine and strong drink, it was one of the few places to get breakfast without having the leftover drunkards from the night before pestering one for money.

The food was often fresh and the help was usually very pleasant. The help looked clean and were mannered servants indeed. MaZak and Dartego grabbed a plate of scrambled eggs and smoked ham, with a stein of fresh goat milk before heading out to setup their booth. Goat milk with a hint of sugar cane delighted their bellies.

The streets were very busy that morning with owners scurrying from place to place preparing to display all of their goods for sell or trade. *Seekers* from the surrounding villages had already peered out into the market to get the first glance as to what was new. They were eyeing new things and making deals before the so-called outsiders (anyone that did not dwell in the Land of the *Seekers*) piled in. This severely crowded the village, and kept a constant haze of dust in the air.

Guards were dressed with gold-colored chest plates and light blue cloth, with matching shin and forearm guards, and semi-helmets covering the crown of their heads. Holding long wooden spears with swords latched at their sides, they were found spread out among the market over the space of a mile. They were stiff, muscular men, which stood as statues throughout the market.

Anyplace items of interest and money were found, security was of necessity. They were the soldiers of Xima the governor, who most humbly required ten percent of all sales plus an upfront cost of ten pieces of Erdian silver per booth, in addition to ten percent tax already on every business which was operated in Trachten.

As the day progressed, the crests of many dignitaries could be seen as the mass of people grew by the minute. MaZak and Dartego saw many familiar faces of those from past buyers. They even took notice of some of the *Sealed* walking among the *seekers*. Soon the stretch would be elbow-to-elbow with people of various ethnic and cultural backgrounds with one thing in mind; *I want the best item for the cheapest price.*

§　　　§　　　§　　　§

By the time mid-day arrived, the mile stretch of booths was overrun with people as expected. Men, women, boys, and girls wandered about searching high and low for the one thing they just can't do without. Everything from armor to clothing, tools to gadgets, games to toys, can be bought or traded at the market. Along with fortune-tellers and medicine-men, there were the kissing booths, storytelling, and all sorts of religious and non-religious professions from mystic to witch, theist to atheist. If one wanted it, someone had it. Seek it there and one would find it.

The crowd was almost overbearingly loud, but from a distance, MaZak could almost swear he heard screams. *There it is again.* Instantly he paused, ending the conversation with a young man questioning him concerning one of his daggers. He did his best to block out the noise nearest him, trying to concentrate on the sounds he believed he heard from the distance.

This time he heard a multitude of hollering and so did Dartego. It was coming from the other end of the far stretch of booths as two of Xima's soldiers pass by, darting through the crowd in that direction. Jerking himself from concentration, he watched the soldiers run past his booth.

"*Gottlos*," was the cry, as panic surfaced in the mind of many. Some dropped what they were looking at and began to run, while others ran, holding what they had. At least they tried to run, but there was no room to move. Thousands of people tried to funnel down the narrow way, seemingly caged in by the continual booths lined along both sides the complete distance, leading to mass confusion.

Men and women began to trample the small children who were unable to get out of the way. Babies were dropped in the mass hysteria, as men and teenagers pushed against the women causing them to stumble and fall. The *Gottlos* were coming, but the *Ubils* were already here. Weapons were drawn, and people carried by the chaos began to fight one another while trying to escape for fear of what was coming. Souls seemed to lose all conciseness of humanity, while focusing purely on self-preservation.

MaZak and Dartego took off behind the booths, running toward the screams as most people remained in the street. Swords in hand, they prepared their minds for battle for whatever sort it would be. As the crowd pushed and shoved their way far from the cries, glimpses of soldiers, members of the *Sealed*, and independent militias were seen running toward the *Gottlos*.

Balls of fire, the size of wagons, fell from the sky, engulfing groups of people at a time. Dignitaries ran for safety as they used their slaves and soldiers as shields for protection. Booths exploded on both sides of the street, sending scraps of burning wood and molten metals through the air like arrows into the flesh of panic-stricken people.

The smell of burning flesh along with torched wood and materials, with sweat, fear, and screams, filled the air most sourly. The fires were hot and suffocated the people as they screamed and ran franticly trying to escape. Flames and smoke made it difficult to see where to go, but the masses continued to sway here and there looking for a way out, fighting each other in their fear to escape.

MaZak saw a small child crying amidst the middle of the path. He was yards away as a burst of adrenalin boosted him toward her. She was afraid, alone, standing still, looking all around. She held her hands out as people ran by without noticing. Her tears dampened her face, and the smoke burned her tender blue eyes. She was nearly six, with curly locks of the lightest blonde hair. He feared she would be trampled by the crowd if he did not reach her. *Almost there*, he thought.

So close, he was but a couple of feet from her. Fighting against the crowd, he pushed people out of his way to reach her. He tripped before he could reach her. A flame, hurled from the sky, licked the surface of the earth, taking the child and all that was with it. He saw it flash before his eyes, but could do nothing.

MaZak's hand reached out as the tips of his fingers began to bubble into blisters. He was too late. *No*, he wanted to scream. Disheartened, it momentarily killed his motivation. He knew there was no time to ponder, but still it was taken. He was hurt, both physically and emotionally, but it would not hinder him from moving to help the people from the attack.

"MaZak," screamed Dartego, running to help up his friend. "The *Gottlos* are too many and you know the *Ubils* are causing most of this hysteria. We've got to fall back and try to regroup with the other *Sealed* and the militias. I'm not sure how many soldiers Xima really has, but we need to find them too!"

MaZak turned to face Dartego with strained redness in his eyes. "The *Dragon* has come. You must hurry to tell our families in Nesal, and warn the other villages on the way. I fear we are not prepared. Call to the *Sealed* in every village. Make sure Ciafus knows of this first. Tell him to prepare for the *Ekleipsis. Rubicund* has surfaced!"

"I will not leave you here. This is too much for the both of us," argued Dartego.

"Let me find the others and…" He was cut off as MaZak grabbed Dartego's shoulder tightly.

"You will go now Dartego!" screamed MaZak.

Dartego was shaken for a moment, as everything except MaZak's voice went silent. "The whole realm including our village is in danger – you must warn them!" exclaimed MaZak.

Speechless, Dartego looked, knowing he must leave to warn the others, yet felt as though he was turning his back on his most beloved friend. The look in MaZak's eyes, a look of concern and fear, Dartego had not seen in many years.

"I shall see you on the other side. May God grant you speed and safety," MaZak claimed as he turned and ran toward the *Gottlos*, baring his sword in his wounded hand.

*Rubicund*, the *Ekleipsis*, echoed in Dartego's head. Fear tried to overtake him, but he would not allow it. Running around the outside of the booths, he ran toward the stables.

*What is that? A sand storm*, he stopped and his mouth dropped. He had never seen a swirling of sand so great.

Far in the distance, from the south, a dark cloud of obvious sand looked like a large storm approaching the city of Palvolin with enormous speed and force. Moving at remarkable speed, Dartego knew there was no escape for the people. The people were closed in with the *Gottlos* to their rear and the storm approaching to their front. It appeared the people would rather weather the storm, for they continued to run head long into it.

*This is indeed a dark day. May God help us*, Dartego thought.

From the storm came an unusual flame, along with the hint of dark wings on either side. From amidst the dust Dartego could almost see a disturbing face with deep green eyes, large smoking nostrils, and jaws wide open exposing fierce teeth. Moving at a tremendous speed, its wings almost touching the ground, powering them up and down against gravity, the beast was coming, projecting himself as an arrow toward Palvolin. It's *Rubicund*.

*Enormous* is too small of a word to describe him, *majestic* not worthy enough to be used. He was a dark red beast with smoke flowing from his nostrils, with wings that extended past both sides of the market, and a tail swinging left to right as he came closer. If not so horrid, indeed he would be a most breathless sight to watch.

His massive jaws held razor sharp teeth spewing forth fire from his gut. Covered in thick plates, he flinched not at the spears and arrows being thrown his way. A chilling sound came forth from his vocal chords as he came into sight. Flames evaporated everything in his path. The force of the wind that followed his swooping upward, threw forcibly to the ground those the fire had not touched, almost putting out the burning flames with the wind.

People recovered and were running all over getting no where. Making it to the stables, Dartego pulled down the first saddle he came to and quickly threw it on the fastest looking horse he saw. *I'll have to settle if we live through this*, he thought.

Mounting the horse, he held the reigns with one hand and gripped tightly his sword with the other. Slowly making his way through the people, trying his best to keep from trampling them with the horse, he glanced over his shoulder to see the destruction gaining on him.

*Gottlos* by the hundreds, cutting and slashing at the people, some being held off by members of the *Sealed*, militias, and soldiers of Xima, while others were free to slay the innocent. Flames and smoke filled the air, and caused his view to be hazed, as he searched for the slightest glimpse of MaZak. A desire to turn and help slowed his emergence past the crowd. Torn between helping his friend and what he knew he must do, burdened his heart and twisted his stomach.

*There, I see him.* Amidst the smoke he saw MaZak carrying what appeared to be two children in his arms, maybe eight or nine years old. *He is still alive.* Covered in soot, they were coughing and holding on for dear life. A glimpse of hope, it was enough to empower him to ride, to ride to Signum to tell Ciafus, then to Nesal to warn the villagers.

Above him flew *Rubicund*, a fierce and evil creature few had seen and lived to tell about. Circling above the people with blazes spewing from its muscular jaws, the bold dark red *Dragon* showed no mercy, with his powerful wings swirling the smoke and fire around like tornados. Some of the *Gottlos* even fell victim to the inferno of the flying beast, but it ceased not from its destruction of Palvolin and the *seekers* there for the market.

A tall, burly *Gottlo* pulled an arrow from his quiver. Filthy, his clothes looked as if they were left sitting in the dirt during a rain. His hands were large with every crack and fingernail holding grit. The muscles in his arms drew the string with ease. The wood bent, leaving only the sharpened arrow head made of stone extending past the bow, resting on the pointer of his fist. He took a breath to steady himself. His aim was fixed, he was ready.

"Stop!" shouted Vikadore, as he placed his enormous hand on the *Gottlo*. Immediately the *Gottlo's* aim was dropped and the draw of the bow was loosened. The *Gottlo* faced Vikadore as if questioning the order.

Larger, in every way, than the *Gottlo* he touched, Vikadore was the captain of the *Gottlos*. His face was full of thick wrinkles embedded with muck, and his eyes drooped with broad bushy brows. He stood likely seven-four towering over most. It would take two men to carry such a sword as his, and never has one been so brave to challenge him. His voice was deep and rough, as if he lived with a constant state of asthma, "Jagare has commanded that one be allowed to live. Come. Return to the slaughter."


Striding from the village, Dartego firmly pressed the horse to its limits. The wind to his face, forcing away the smoke with every breath feeling fresher, he dared not look back. Emotions of anger, fear, sympathy, and anxiousness filled his mind as he rode. Questions, answers, tradition, folklore, King Salvare, the *Book of Wisdom* all came together in the midst of his thoughts, from things learned over the years necessary to separate fact from fiction. *God help us! Please send the King.*

# *Choices*

arly morning came with dew and the smell of fresh air. The sun was barely awake, with only a small halo appearing over the oaks and sycamores of Nesal, while faint hints of light played peek-a-boo amidst the trees. The village was quiet but for the rustlings of three teenagers getting dressed and saddling their horses. It appeared Rayhold had convinced Vandor and Kayla to accompany him to see Cenobia in Qualtes.

Yawning still, they mounted their horses, mostly speaking in grunts and nods. It would take quite a while to travel south to Qualtes, so they made sure to pack themselves loaves of bread, goat cheese, some jerky, and a full water pouch each. They would enjoy the time together; it was just too early to think of such things.

The sun finally decided to show its face as the three began to awaken more. The trip so far had been silent till it was broken by Kayla. "So Rayhold, how long have you liked Cenobia?"

"Uh," caught off guard, "I found her very nice when I came with my father to purchase some animal hides a while back. I just thought it would be nice if you both could meet her and she could meet you two."

"Indeed it would be nice to meet your friend," replied Kayla.

"I am glad that we are able to spend some time together today. It seems it has been a while since we all have enjoyed a good day," added Vandor.

"That is true. What have you been spending your time with Rayhold? We haven't seen much of you lately," asked Kayla.

"Yes Rayhold, I have missed our sparring," added Vandor.

"I have been helping my parents a lot lately. I too am glad of today," answered Rayhold.

They paused for a short time near a small stream. The air was full of the songs of birds and the flowing water. They sat on the soft, thick grass, leaning back against large smooth rocks. Small talk between bites of bread, cheese, and jerky with the occasional drink of water filled the time. Only a quick break and they were back on the trail to Qualtes.

Arriving in Qualtes before noon, the village was somewhat busy. The small market where people brought their vegetables and fruits, clothes and linens, handcrafts and such, was crowded with onlookers. Buying, selling, and trading were a common thing among people, especially in the smaller villages. In this, they all helped each other survive by also building relationships with one another.

There she stood as they entered the village. Rayhold saw her almost instantly. He pointed Cenobia out to Vandor and Kayla, but asked them not to make themselves obvious by staring. They concurred and dismounted their horses at a common horse post, made of eight-inch pine crossbeams, attached to twelve-inch legs, evenly spaced the length of ten yards or so. It was meant as a place for visitors to tie their horses and the like while they visited the village.

As they walked toward Cenobia standing by her family's vegetable stand, she turned to face them. "Rayhold," she said in a surprised tone.

He fidgeted and replied, "Hello, Cenobia."

Looking at Rayhold, she did not really notice Vandor and Kayla. "It's been a while, how have you been?"

"I've been well," he acknowledged. Pointing to each, "These are my friends Vandor and Kayla," he disclosed.

Vandor extended his hand, followed by Kayla.

"Vandor and I want to look around, so we'll back later," Kayla said, giving Rayhold a chance to talk to Cenobia.

Vandor and Kayla walked off among the crowd of the booths, looking around to see what was being sold. Rayhold and Cenobia walked over to where they had tied the horses, with Cenobia's mother's permission, of course. It was apparent to any that paid attention, that they were excited to see one another. Eager to share their thoughts, they sat and spoke for hours.

It soon came time that they must leave to make it back to Nesal before dark. It was enough that their parents had allowed them to travel with the fear of *Gottlos* sightings here and there throughout the land of Erde. Although they had not been seen this far east, there was always the possibility in the mind of their parents. These three had not even seen such a thing as the *Gottlos* so they seemed but as tales to scare children.

"I must be going soon Cenobia, so that we make it back before dark," told Rayhold.

"I am so glad you came," Cenobia replied.

In his mind he fought with the idea of whether or not to give her the amulet from Onyx. Decided, pulling it from his pocket, he opened the cloth around it and handed it to Cenobia. "I have brought you a gift."

She was delighted and her face showed as much. "It is beautiful Rayhold."

He was happy that she was pleased. There was a slight discomfort within him in giving it to her because he knew the power behind it. If worn, he would never know her true feelings, for the amulet would control them. He questioned the motive, but dared not take the chance at loss. She appeared to like him, so it really wasn't forcing her to go against her will in his mind.

She put the necklace on and instantly Rayhold could swear he saw a quick glimmer in her eyes. "I love you Rayhold."

He was startled and amazed, *It must be working*, he pondered. At a loss for words for the moment he fumbled, "I… You do?"

"Yes Rayhold. I would not say it if I did not mean it," she replied.

Vandor and Kayla walked up, breaking the conversation. "We better be getting back," Vandor acknowledged.

Cenobia held Rayhold tightly, "I shall await your return."

Rayhold and Cenobia stood as they all moved toward the horses.

Leaving the village, Cenobia watched them until they were out of sight. Rayhold made sure to wave and keep eye contact for as long as he could see her. He really did like her, maybe not as purely as Vandor and Kayla did each other, but did so nevertheless. It was just his fear of loss that compelled him to do such, or so he told himself as they rode off.

Small talk again filled their time back to Nesal. While Rayhold and Cenobia had sat mostly near the horse post, leaving for a while to show Rayhold around the village and grab a bite to eat and fresh water, Vandor and Kayla had slowly passed through looking at every little thing each booth had to offer. Vandor had taken the little money he did have and bought Kayla a nice leather bracelet with daisies on it which tied at the bottom.

Coming into sight was the same small stream they had passed in the morning. Their mouths were dry, so the decided it would be nice to take a small break before continuing on. They had the time, and agreed to stop for a moment or two.

There was noise from above them, but they were too slow to get out of the way. Down came a large creature with the appearance of a man. With the likeness of a beast, it was larger than most men and smelled of decay. These three had not seen the like in their lives until then.

Landing almost atop Kayla, the creature wrapped his arms around her as they tumbled from the horse toward the ground. Instinctively, she closed her eyes and gritted her teeth as they fell: a thump as they hit, with a cry of pain from Kayla on impact. Completely caught off guard, Vandor and Rayhold were stunned as it happened. The creature lay on his back, taking the blunt of the fall, while Kayla kicked wildly, using her strength to push against his grasp.

The creature stood holding Kayla tightly around her folded arms, which were bent covering her chest, with one arm, while holding a knife near her face with its other hand. Kayla's feet dangled in the air. She grunted and continuously kicked and pushed against his grip, trying to free herself. It was useless, for the creature was too strong for a teenage girl. If she would have only considered reaching for her dagger, she may have been able to escape.

Quickly Vandor and Rayhold dismounted. Vandor drew his sword, a little delayed, still getting used to a full blade and sheath. Running toward this fierce beast with the point of his sword forward, Vandor screamed, "Release her!"

Rayhold did not pull his dagger, but stared at the creature for a moment. As if being summoned from the depths of his very soul, instinctively Rayhold called upon the sorcery of Onyx. His eyes whitened, his body stilled, as the control of unknown strength and power, as if borrowed from another, seemed to flow through his vessels of life. He crossed his arms out in front of him in an 'X' formation. His muscles flexed and tightened as he fought against what seemed to be merely the air. Drops of sweat dribbled down Rayhold's sideburns, as he gritted his teeth with force.

As Rayhold pulled his arms out of the 'X' formation, the arms of the beast seemed to shake and lose strength. Gradually the arms of the creature released Kayla. The arms of the beast were supernaturally controlled by Rayhold. The beast felt the dark power upon him, the influence he knew too well, as Kayla jerked herself away from the attacker. The knife fell away from Kayla to the ground. Kayla ran from the beast, as he stared at the three teenagers.

Vandor was stunned for a moment, seeing Rayhold perform such a task. *It is sorcery.* The law had been ingrained by his father Tindal, *such is against the law.*

Glancing between the three, the creature chose to turn and run. Rayhold lowered his arms as the creature showed a moment of shock. Rayhold's eyes returned to their color, while the magnificent feeling of power subsided back to whence it came. "Vandor slay it with your sword," yelled Rayhold.

Vandor could not bring himself to do it. The creature was running away and he cared more to see if Kayla was alright. Between the creature and Kayla, Vandor's eyes shifted. The beast was slow, but mowed through the brush toward the thick woods. Kayla lay upon the ground, propped upon her hip and elbow, panting, watching the beast run away. Vandor's heart moved him to Kayla's side, looking into her eyes, seeing the fear which dwelt there.

A scream, a terrible noise, coming from the creature's direction, caused Vandor and Kayla to look back toward the beast. It fell forward with a thud, sliding a little, knocking down the underbrush. *What is that in its back?* It was Rayhold's dagger protruding from the center of the beast's shoulder blades. They could hear it still breathing horrific gasps of air; the creature was mortally wounded, unable to move, assumingly paralyzed, yet not dead.

Rayhold walked toward the beast, while Vandor and Kayla seemed to be frozen in time, merely watching their friend with amazement. Rayhold seemed to approach the beast with confidence, as though he had seen and slain these types many times before. The only humanity this beast appeared to contain was the fear which could be seen in his eyes as Rayhold came near. Placing his hand atop the beast's head, covering its solemn face, Rayhold muttered forbidden words, of an unlawful dialect. A flash of bright light flickered from the cracks between Rayhold's hand and the beast's forehead. The body of the beast jerked then stilled in silence. Rayhold withdrew his blade from the beast, stood, and simply observed the fallen foe.

The events happened so fast, catching them most unaware, being extremely out of the ordinary. Vandor and Kayla were still not completely sure as to what they had witnessed. Vandor helped Kayla up. She had a few bruises, but over all she was fine. Kayla picked up her bow and quiver. Vandor sheathed his sword and helped Kayla pick up her loose arrows, and then they walked over to where Rayhold was standing.

"What is that? Is that a man?" asked Vandor.

Without lifting his eyes, "A *Gottlo*," responded Rayhold.

"A *Gottlo*? How do you know? Have you ever seen one," questioned Vandor.

"I just know." Rayhold turned to look at Vandor, "You should have used your sword."

"It was running away. Why not let it go?" questioned Vandor.

"We must kill the enemy before they kill us Vandor. If we were to let it live, it may decide to hunt us down another day," he explained.

To Vandor's knowledge, none of them had seen such a being nor had ever encountered true combat, and definitely not actual bloodshed and death. Vandor pondered how Rayhold could be so cold and eager to kill without even the slightest hint of fear or cautiousness.

Kayla, holding herself with her arms, not wanting to go near the *Gottlo*, said, "Rayhold, what did you do?"

"I killed him Kayla," replied Rayhold.

She looked again to the beast, with the smell of the vile creature still upon her curling her stomach. Rayhold knew that was not what she was talking about. "Rayhold, I mean what did you do to have him release me?"

"You used sorcery," Vandor interrupted.

"I...You mustn't tell anyone," Rayhold exclaimed.

"It's unlawful Rayhold," Vandor interjected.

"Yes Vandor. That is why you mustn't say a word about it to anyone," pleaded Rayhold.

They argued back and forth a time, questioning Rayhold as he continued to defend himself, always returning that it was the sorcery which allowed Kayla to live. They kept reminding him that sorcery was against the law, Tindal's father often spoke of it, and King Salvare himself had condemned such. Rayhold argued it was no different than the power the *seers* used, whereas Vandor and Kayla assured him the difference was where the power originated, from the very hand of God or the *Darkness* which fought against Him. He conceded that he had learned it from a *pale* named Onyx, who made him swear to secrecy concerning it.

They ceased from argument, but the discussion was far from settled. Could they tell of the slaying of the *Gottlo* without the mentioning of sorcery? If this was indeed a *Gottlo* and they told not, what if there were others? Was Nesal in danger? Surely they would never be able to leave Nesal again.

Sorcery was punishable by death, and if told, Rayhold's fate would be sealed. Vandor knew his father was too strict, but Rayhold was his friend. Could his father, Tindal, show mercy if Rayhold swore to refrain from such?

Many questions in their minds kept the trip back quiet. They had agreed to keep silent of the *Gottlo* and sorcery till they could come to a safe way to approach the subject. With the burden of knowing something which could not be shared, their hearts were heavy.

# Hope in Signum

*D*artego had been riding north across Trachten to Signum. Pausing for only moments along the way, he warned those in Xiacon of what had occurred in Palvolin. As soldiers prepared in Xiacon to seek out Xima in Palvolin, Dartego continued over the Umeten Canal toward Kirche in Signum as fast as he could. This was much for a man of his age, but the will to save the souls of Erde from the *Darkness* moved Dartego to press on.

§      §      §      §

Kirche was an established castle and school named after its founder Erdessest Kirche, where the *Sealed* were trained in the wisdom and arts of the *King*. It was an enormous castle made of individual stones three stories high, built in the place where King Salvare's kingdom once stood. It was surrounded by a twenty foot stone wall, three feet wide, circling the castle, with a gate which took six men to move.

When Judarius murdered King Salvare, one of his first acts was to clean out the *King's* castle. Most of the *Sealed* had fled from Signum, so at the death of Judarius, enraged with malice, Galtare and his band of *Gottlos* destroyed the *King's* castle. Their desire was to rid the land of Erde of all remembrance of King Salvare. Had it been possible, they would have succeeded.

Erdessest had convinced men from all over Erde to build a new castle in Signum for the return of King Salvare during the *Awakening*. They experienced a small amount of freedom, per se, to rebuild during the years Galtare remained in *Oscuridad*, as if oblivious to outside the walls of his castle. Galtare lay sickly unto death, while the hearts of the people of Erde moved back toward the *King*.

Jagare had the desire to retake Signum at his father Galtare's death, and was upon his march toward such thoughts, when he was dealt the deadly blow to his head. Though the bowman never found, the voices of Erde cheered none the less. Jagare had been silent since that day, as the stories whether Jagare was dead or merely awaiting a time to resurface carried from village to village, among the breeze, throughout Erde.

Erdessest, already great in years, fell asleep soon after its completion.

§ § § §

Dartego was old and his body told him so. This ride was almost unbearable. Many times he felt the need to stop, only to recall the words of MaZak, "The *Dragon* has come. You must hurry to tell our families in Nesal, and warn the other villages on the way. I fear we are not prepared. Call to the *Sealed* in every village. Make sure Ciafus knows of this first. Tell him to prepare for the *Ekleipsis*. *Rubicund* has surfaced!"

§ § § §

*Ekleipsis*: Judarius claimed that darkness would one day overcome and destroy all light. The name of that day, he called thus. True, there was a span of *Dark Ages* for the land of Erde during the reign of Galtare, but that which Judarius spoke of was a complete annihilation of the remembrance of all which is pure and good.

Galtare had even claimed that he had brought in the *Ekleipsis*, but the *Awakening* had proven him wrong. His reign had brought forth the *Dark Ages* which Judarius had set in motion, causing many to lose hope, but the flicker of light remained. It was but a pre- *Ekleipsis* or false- *Ekleipsis*, depending on the person; that was merely a glimpse of what could come to pass. Some used it as proof that a true total *Ekleipsis* was not possible, while others saw it as proof to what would happen if people lost sight of all that the *King* spoke of.

Dartego and the *Sealed* believed the latter, and thus anxiously awaited the return of the *King*, to put an end to the *Darkness* forever.

§        §        §        §

Days had passed with Dartego and his borrowed horse growing weary past exhaustion. With Signum in sight he pulled the last bit of his strength, pressing the horse to move faster. The wind blew hard against his bearded face and bushy brows. Squinting, he could see Kirche in the distance. His bones ached, his back was stiff, and his stomach growled of hunger, but the sight of the *King's* insignia upon the walls of Kirche sprang forth life within his bosom. Dartego longed for the sweet rest he knew he would find once there. The comfort and care he knew the *Sealed* would greet him with caused him to will the thoroughbred to stride beneath him with purpose.

A jerk, a stumble, Dartego could feel his horse sway to one side. It appeared slow in his mind, but only seconds in reality. The horse's front hoof had found a random hole in the plain less than a mile from Kirche. Impulse moved Dartego to prepare for the fall that awaited him. How could this be but moments from where he needed to be? The horse could not regain his balance, nor hold up the weight upon his back. The fall was inevitable. Dartego could do nothing to save himself from it.

At full speed the horse pounded the ground, shoulder then head, twisting and flipping, with Dartego tangled amidst it all. Dartego was beat by the body of the horse and the ground as they rolled and tumbled multiple times. Grunts and moans filled Dartego's mouth and emptiness filled his mind, as they stopped.

Dust rose, forming a cloud. The horse was lifeless on its side. Dartego was motionless, lying face down with his legs under the horse. The dust settled back to the ground, mixing with drops of blood. Shall they have come this far, but to die?

Eyes saw it all from outside the walls of Kirche, including a few of the *Sealed.* There was no doubt that such a fall could kill even the strongest and best riders. Labat and his two sons rushed in Dartego's direction. They and their horses were fresh and moved like the wind, covering the distance in minutes. They knew nothing of this man but that he needed help.

Labat, a *Sealed* veteran of fifteen years, dismounted his horse as he arrived at the incident. His twin sons, Falken and Ion, tall muscular fellows, followed suit. Recently turning twenty, they had been numbered among the *Sealed* for nearly two years. Still in training, but had grasped the teaching well.

They found Dartego mumbling something they could not quite make out. Shrugging, they worked to roll the dead horse from his legs. His face held small cuts, but they worried more about the gash atop the large lump upon his forehead. Drool hung from his mouth as he repeated incoherent phrases over and over. They could see his legs look crushed, but were sure internal problems most likely also existed. They needed to get him back to Kirche to the physician.

Entering the walls of Kirche, they were met at the door by the medical team, led by Nartod. A dark man with gray wisdom covering his head and face, he was one of the first to come to Kirche, as it was being built, and was now over the infirmary.

"Dartego," Nartod looked surprised, recognizing the man.

"You know him?" asked Labat.

"Quite so. This man was among us before even I."

Labat and his sons informed Nartod of what they had seen and that Dartego had been mumbling phrases they could not decipher. Nartod then led four other men carrying the stretcher holding Dartego to the medical wing. They would care for him as best they could.

Nartod and the four men had managed to clean and bandage Dartego, so he was now resting on a cot in one of the four bays they had for various conditions: one for the sick; one for recoverable injuries; another for harsher wounds; and then one for the least likely to recover. To Nartod, it looked bad. Considering Dartego's age and the incident, it did not leave much promise for recovery. Yet Nartod acknowledged he had seen miracles before. As such, he would try to remain hopeful.

Nartod turned to leave the room when he heard movement. He turned to see Dartego sit strait up. Eyes wide open, "*Ekleipsis,*" Dartego said clearly.

Nartod was speechless. The hairs on Nartod's neck stood up as a chill raced down his back. Dartego coughed and fell back. His eyes rolled to the back of his head as air exited his lungs. He went to sleep to be with his fathers. There was nothing Nartod could do. Unable to revive Dartego, Nartod ran to find the Auctoritas.

§   §   §   §

The Auctoritas was the Commander of the *Sealed*, not as a king would be, but as a commander nominated by the *Sealed*, approved by the council, and then voted on by the *Sealed* as a group.

There were a few requirements for being an Auctoritas: He must be at least the age of thirty and be no older than sixty at the time of vote. He must also have served as one of the *Sealed* for a minimum of ten years. He must remain at Kirche during his time in office (as a home, not physically unable to leave).

He was to be a figure head for what is right, not above the people, but for the people. Being approved by the council, he could also be removed by the council, due to clear variance and departure from the *Book of Wisdom*. The *Sealed* believe they have one true king who is King Salvare, so none dare assume the title of such in his absence.

The current Auctoritas was Ciafus. Ciafus was a young man in his early fifties of strong build, with a solid jaw of truth, with piercing eyes as one that could look through the lies of another. Upon the leave of MaZak, years ago, he had been given the title of Auctoritas concerning the *Sealed*.

With unanimous approval from the council, along with a majority vote of ninety percent among the *Sealed*, it has placed Ciafus in authority till he either chooses to step down, dies, or upon the return of King Salvare. He dared not rule as one that is above all men, as a *Popish*, but merely as one that others may look to in times of danger and support.

The *Sealed* were free to live as they saw right, as long as by the guidelines set forth by King Salvare in his *Book of Wisdom*, without special permission from Ciafus. He was there not as a dictator or legalist but to hold the common interest of the *King*, that the *Sealed* be not persuaded to waver from such.

The council was made of twelve men who were also voted in by the *Sealed*. As with the office of Auctoritas, so were the qualifications for the council members. Known as the Council of Kirche, these were the current members in alphabetical order: Adevar, Bron van Vreugde, Ehrlich, Frieden, Fuerza, Langmutig, Odvaha, Pameten, Rakkaus, Usk, Vitis, and Zavest. Bron van Vreugde was the eldest of the council, with Adevar the youngest.

§   §   §   §

Nartod ran the flight of stairs rather quickly, making his way to the center of the castle on the second floor. Reaching the council room he pushed through the door. Ciafus set at the far end head of the long, thick, wooden table with maps and papers spread the length thereof. Sitting on like-padded chairs, as Ciafus, was Adevar, Usk, Ehrlich, Pameten, Vitis, and Odvaha to his left, with Fuerza, Zavest, Rakkaus, Frieden, Langmutig, and Bron van Vreugde to his right. An extravagant rug covered the floor of the enormous room with paintings and tapestries decorating the walls.

Ciafus, Usk, and Bron van Vreugde stood most serious. Nartod paused to catch his breath, looking into a group of inquisitive eyes. "Dear Nartod, this is most unlike you to barge in when such a meeting is being held. Could this not wait?" questioned Bron van Vreugde.

"He looks most pale, Bron. Speak Nartod, what have you to tell us?" Ciafus inquired.

"The *Ekleipsis*, dear Ciafus," said Nartod almost yelling, yet breathless.

The room silenced. "The *Ekleipsis*?" repeated Ciafus, more as a question.

Nartod moved forward to gain support from the table as he caught his breath. It was not so much the run, but the thoughts that accompanied him up the stairs that worked him. He told the council of Dartego and the accident, how he was brought inside the castle, and spoke only one word before he fell asleep. "*Ekleipsis*." He told how Dartego had come from the direction of Trachten, which was due north of the *Shadow Lands* and *Oscuridad*. They all knew that which he spoke of, they just could not believe that it was spoken.

# Secrets Revealed

*A* pounding at the door awakened Sycress. Her eyes sprung open with the jar of the noise. She rolled over to shake Labo whispering, "Labo…Labo…Someone is at the door…wake up." He was stubborn and deep asleep, not even flinching at her call. She found his ribs among his chubby sides and poked them. A flinch as hoped.

Labo tiredly questioned Sycress for waking him. It was a little past midnight so this was most uncommon behavior from her. Before she was able to answer, the pounding came again. Startling Labo, he jumped to his feet, sliding on his pants and grabbing an odd-shaped black handled dagger by his bed.

The pounding continued as he reached the door slowly. "Who is it?" Labo questioned loud and deep.

"The council," returned the quick reply. (This council was the Council of Nesal, made of seven persons.) The speaker was Tindal and tonight he had led the group to Labo's home, but that was not who they sought.

*The council*, Labo questioned to himself and reluctantly opened the door, hiding the dagger inside his jacket that hung near the window.

The first person Labo saw was Tindal carrying a lantern, but none of the council looked very happy in the least. He felt the nerves come alive throughout his body, not really sure as to why the men were here or why they looked so. *What would drive them from their beds at this hour,* he did not know and it scared him. Guilty conscience or human nature, he couldn't help but run things through his mind to see if he had done something worthy of the visit.

"Labo, is Rayhold here?" Tindal asked without introduction or common chat. Straight to the point relieved Labo of his question if it was he, only to create new fear by the mere mention of his son's name.

Sycress had heard every word as if she had the ears of God and made haste to make herself descent to be seen among men. She spilled from the room, directly to the door, asking before words could leave Labo's mouth. "What do you need with our son?" she asked intently, feeling the motherly instinct of protection overtaking her.

§    §    §    §

Although Vandor and Rayhold were friends, less close most recently, their parents were not so much. Rayhold's parents, Labo and Sycress, were quiet people that were hardly seen in Nesal, as most of the things they sold were delivered to other villages. When they were seen, there were mostly common greetings and such without much more.

Vandor's parents, Tindal and Sorie, on the other hand, took part in other things. Tindal spent most of his time in study, teaching, and learning of history and other topics. He was speaker of the council, so he was close to family and the council members, but not many others. Sorie was quiet and mingled mostly with those she had known for years.

§    §    §    §

Tindal and the council seemed eager on seeing Rayhold and not really idle chat. "We need to see Rayhold," Tindal demanded, still standing outside the home with the council to his back.

Rayhold was now up and peeking through the crack of his door. He was not really able to see anyone because of the angle, but clearly he heard his name and recognized the voice of Vandor's father Tindal.

Fear gripped him tightly. He pondered a hundred thoughts it seemed. Vandor, Kayla, and he had agreed to refrain from speaking of the incident of a few nights ago. Had they lied? Had they broken down and told on him? Surely they were his friends and would not betray him. But what else could it be, he could not imagine. Their vow kept returning to his mind.

Labo and Sycress held Tindal and the council at the door, questioning and reasoning as to what this was all about. Tiring, Tindal stepped up pushing his way into the house between the two declaring, "By the authority of the Council of Nesal, we demand to see Rayhold your son!"

Labo and Sycress, turned to face him, and cried, "You have no authority in our home," as the council moved forward anyway.

Labo shoved Tindal in the back screaming, "You have no authority," as Sycress backed up in fear, echoing the same.

Tindal fell forward to the ground dropping the lantern. Qad and Kol rushed in, grabbing hold of Labo, pinning him to the wooden wall with a loud thump, for Labo was a large man. Nau moved to hold Sycress back, less aggressively than the others had Labo, as Rayhold ran from his room.

"Leave them alone. Here am I," cried out Rayhold, facing them all.

As Tindal recovered himself from the floor, the two men tightly held Labo, and now Sycress sat with Nau near her.

Yanes stood in the doorway while Ishbal and Zoac, holding shackles, moved to the sides of Rayhold. Rayhold knew they had come for him, but stood in place. He moved his sight between Tindal, his father, and his mother. He could see the anger, fear, and hurt in their eyes. He pondered the idea of running, but decided against it. Rayhold's mind was too cluttered to think.

He didn't resist as they placed the shackles around his wrists and ankles. They were cold, hard, and rang out a metallic sound when closed. Zoac then locked the chain connecting the wrists shackles to the ankle ones. Rayhold regretfully looked down at his bonds, then upward to Tindal, "What have I done?" Though his use of sorcery came quickly to mind, his pride cried out, *I am innocent.* Knowing the use of sorcery now would seal his fate in death, he withheld from such.

Straight-faced and emotionless, Tindal replied, "A witness came forth tonight telling us of a surety that you have conducted acts of sorcery."

Arguments came both from Labo and Sycress that their son did not even know of such. Qad and Kol doubled their strength, pressing against Labo to keep him held. Nau pressed Sycress firmly but gently on the shoulder as she appeared to make an attempt to get up from the chair. Tindal demanded silence. Only Rayhold was to speak to the allocation of his actions. Rayhold was silent.

"Rayhold, how do you answer the charges of sorcery?" Tindal questioned.

"I…" Rayhold glanced to his father then took a long look at his mother. He was torn between thoughts: The look of anger in the eyes of his father, and the hurt in the tears of his mother. If Vandor and Kayla had betrayed him, then he could merely claim it was used to save their lives and even the village from the *Gottlo*, which may offer some chance of leniency. If they had not mentioned it and it was another, it could pull Vandor and Kayla into the issue at hand, only adding to his affliction.

Rayhold remained still, as if calm to the situation, but on the inside, he trembled in fear. "I neither affirm nor deny the charges," Rayhold decided.

None were too delighted in his answer, so they did what must be done according to the law of Nesal. They led him from his home to the bars of silence beneath the council seat of Nesal. The six followed Tindal's lead as Labo held Sycress, forcibly restraining himself against his desire to slay them all to free his son. They watched the council take away their son into darkness, listening to the sounds of the shackles and chains echoing through the village. While Sycress worried what would become of her son, Labo pondered thoughts of how to free him.

One accused of sorcery must face the council. They must ask the accused of their guilt, whereby the accused must affirm or deny the accusations. Upon affirmation, the accused must be burned alive. If the accused denies the accusations, then all witnesses and the accused must appear before the council to determine if indeed the accusations are truthful, and if indeed sorcery has truly been used or studied by the accused. If the accused is found guilty by the council, the accused is burned alive the same day, if found innocent they are freed but limited to the boundaries of Nesal for the space of six months observation.

§        §        §        §

Yanes, drawing the short straw, was the lucky one to watch over Rayhold till morning. Though guarding, Yanes did not stay down below where the prisoners are kept. Beside the council room, Yanes sat at a small table and chair outside of a door leading to a short passageway, which extends down into the earth. There below was a small hall and three six-by-six cells for individual holdings of accused or guilty persons. No one goes in or out, except the council, without the council's majority permission.

Below the well-furnished and kept council room sat a basement of filth. Not much more than a holding place for a couple of days at the most, there was very little stock put into how it was kept or the environment it held, not to mention the "serves them right" attitude of people toward those which ended up there. This mind-set kept most from even considering the idea of the conditions of such a place they saw themselves as never deserving to be.

Sitting shackled and chained below the council seat of Nesal, Rayhold found himself on a short, poorly padded, wooden table for a bed with two sheets (one slightly thicker than the other), a cat hole for a toilet, and bars to hold him in. Being underground, there was no window and the atmosphere was cool and damp with dirt floors. A lonely candle near the entrance to this waste hole was the only flicker of light seen by those that ended up here.

Staring at the floor, pondering many thoughts in his mind, Rayhold suddenly felt a chill. An odd puff of air blew out the candle and total blackness overwhelmed the basement. Rayhold opened his eyes as wide as he could, but there was no light to give him even the slightest amount of vision. He lifted his hand in front of his face, pulling the chains and his other hand along with it, but was unable to see it as it touched his nose.

Suddenly within his cell, floating mid-air, he saw a circular ball of green light. A glow came from a solid florescent oval core the size of an egg, with sparks and lightning coming forth from the center, encompassing it as if encased in a large invisible sphere. It was beautiful. Its brightness illuminated more and more as the axis appeared to spin faster and faster. Rayhold looked at it intently and reached out to touch it.

As Rayhold touched it, the light became solid green, too bright to directly look at. Squinting away from the sphere, he then saw it was held by a dark figure. He instantly jerked his hand back with the rattle of chains and shackles ringing in his ears. His heart began to pound with fear rising within him. Fear, but of what he was unsure. Was his mind but playing tricks? He was alone down there and there was no entrance but from above where Yanes sat. His mind betrayed his desire of thought and seemed to close down to only a reaction of panic.

"Rayhold," a voice, seemingly from the sphere, called out in a deep whisper.

This did not calm his nerves, but caused more terror to overwhelm him. So much so that he was unable to move. He tried to search the darkness of the shadow, avoiding directly looking into the light which momentarily blinded him. Rapid blinks, trying to focus against the light and on the shadow did little good.

"It is I, Rayhold. Fear not, it is I Onyx," a smooth whisper came forth.

Disbelief and excitement flooded Rayhold's mind all at once. He was fully aware that Onyx knew sorcery, for he had taught him such, but the fact that he stood before him was quite amazing in Rayhold's mind. While sulking in this pit of isolation, he hadn't thought to use the sorcery he had been taught. It had never crossed his mind to cry out to Onyx for help. Maybe it was because sorcery was the very thing that had him here in the first place.

"Can you get me out of here?" Rayhold quietly asked.

"Indeed I can, but first Rayhold, do I have thy allegiance?" growled Onyx.

Startled by the question and still amazed by Onyx's entrance, Rayhold replied, "Yes." Part of Rayhold was answering honestly, yet the other only for the sake of escape from his situation.

"Will ye swear an oath to such?" asked Onyx coldly.

Without thinking Rayhold replied, "Yes, I swear."

Onyx held out his free hand, "By this oath ye swear allegiance to both my master and I?"

Rayhold reached out to Onyx. Very anxious to leave this cell, Rayhold replied, "I swear, I swear," without even asking who this master was that Onyx spoke of. To Rayhold this was merely the means to escape his current predicament, no different than telling his parents he promised to obey to free himself from punishment when caught, only to find himself needing to promise yet again another day. Rayhold figured he would ponder the question of who this master was on the morrow, once he was free to think.

As Onyx's fingers tightened into a grip, Rayhold felt a sharp pain shoot through his arm into his shoulder. He jerked, but Onyx did not release him. The florescent sphere levitated in the air as Onyx placed his other hand over the outside of Rayhold's hand. Rayhold struggled to pull back his hand from Onyx, feeling a hot burning sensation throughout his hand. This time Onyx released him, as Rayhold almost fell backwards.

By instinct, Rayhold covered his hurting hand with his other. Massaging it roughly, he hoped to remove the uncomfortable burning feeling, but it didn't help. Rayhold looked at Onyx, removing his left hand from atop his right. Rayhold looked down at his throbbing hand Onyx had just released. There was now an odd *mark* atop his hand, holding the appearance of having been tattooed into his flesh with black ink. He had seen this *mark* before, upon the *Gottlo* he killed while with Vandor and Kayla.

Onyx reached his hand back to holding the glowing green sphere, "Shall we go then?"

Frustrated, Rayhold replied, "What about…" He was cut off by the sound of the shackles unlocking and dropping to the dirt floor with the chains. Momentarily amazed he asked, "How did you get in here? How do we get out without Yanes seeing us?"

"Have ye learned nothing dear Rayhold? I hold the power to do that which I will," growled Onyx.

Onyx muttered words that Rayhold had not yet been taught. The glow disappeared, returning to total darkness, as they vanished from the slough of bondage beneath the Council of Nesal. Yanes snoozing off and on knew nothing of what had transpired literally under his nose. Likely, he would have been unable to stop it regardless.

§     §     §     §

An individual, wearing a dark grey cloak, crept into the council building, making his way slowly around the side hallway, to the desk where Yanes sat. He was unknowingly guarding the already escaped Rayhold. Hunched over in the chair, Yanes' head rested atop his folded arms on the table. Silence was only broken with the sound of light snores. The cloaked individual moved smoothly toward Yanes as he slept.

Standing aside Yanes, the aggressor drove his dagger deep into the side of Yanes' unprotected ribs with brute force. Yanes gave out a gasp and flinched to the left. His eyes sprang alive in fear. His mouth opened as if to scream, but unable to release any sound. Yanes leaned over, pulling the chair to the ground with him. The cloaked attacker withdrew the dagger and plunged it into Yanes' chest, then pulled it out again turning toward the basement door. Yanes was unconscious as his life flowed from him.

The murderer entered the basement door, and raced down the steps to the three cells, of which one was to hold Rayhold. To his surprise, all three were empty. In a moment of confusion, he paused to physically check the doors to each of the cells. Pulling on the doors, he realized that they were still locked and there was no Rayhold here below. A huff and sigh of surprise, frustration, and confusion seeped out as he returned to the top of the stairs, and headed out the front of the council building.

Around the villages, one by one the council members met like fates, as they were awakened by the pounding on their doors. Assuming another council issue pertaining to earlier matters, their wives did not initially waken and the men did not suspect foul play. Qad, Kol, Ishbal, and Zoac all fell to final sleep at their doorsteps, by the hand of a cloaked assailant. A merciless slaying of vengeance had come to Nesal, or did it exist from within?

A knock at the door had Nau pulling on the pants and boots sitting next to his bed. His wife Amashai pulled the sheets higher as a cool breeze chilled the back of her neck, which had been kept warm lying against Nau. She spoke a little detest of the council calling for her husband again this night, but dosed back to sleep when Nau failed to give a reply.

Opening the door, Nau met the attacker. Unexplainably fast for being woken from his sleep, Nau was swift enough to escape the deadly swing of the dagger he was met with. Slamming his door, it caught the forearm of the invader inside his home. The sting of pressure caused the aggressor to drop the dagger with a grunted squawk of pain.

Doing his best to hold the door with his right shoulder and leg, along with the weight of his body, Nau reached down and grabbed the dropped dagger with his left hand. Gripping the dagger tightly, Nau swung the door back open, lifting the blade mid-waist high. As the door opened and the attacker was struggling to pull away, gravity grabbed the cloaked aggressor pulling him backwards, off balance to the ground. Sparing no time, Nau pounced down upon the attacker with the blade piercing his heart. A groan escaped from the foe as he appeared to grip his chest, but death took him.

Nau felt out of breath and held the dagger in place for a moment to ensure its purpose had been served. The cloaked foe laid still and Nau was sure it was over. He stood to his feet and took notice of the face revealed from the fallen back hood. To his dismay, the face belonged to Labo. Nau's eyes widened in surprise, for he assumed it would be no one from Nesal.

Screams of the slain men's wives began to fill the night air, bringing fear to the children of Nesal, causing them also to cry. The noise broke Nau loose from staring. Nau cried, "Amashai get the children, and bring them to our room."

Pulling his sword, Nau slammed the door and ran to the center of the village, near the council chambers. He rang the warning bell, almost jerking it from the post. Its echo bounced off of the surrounding trees as lights began to appear inside the homes, with the streets already quickly filling with inquisitive people.

Nau left the bell and rushed in to check on Yanes. Not really surprised, but hoping against his fears, he saw Yanes covered in blood spilled out on the floor. Nau ran to Yanes' side, but realized he was too late. There was nothing he could do.

Turning toward the door, he took notice that it was already open. The hole was coal black. He called out, "Rayhold." No answer. "Rayhold, are you down here?"

He grabbed the light on the table where Yanes sat, and headed down the tunnel to the cell Rayhold was placed in. *Gone*, Nau said to himself and yet didn't notice that the cell was still locked.

Making his way back up the small hallway, he was met by Tindal at the door. "He's gone."

Shock gripped Tindal as Nau spoke of meeting Labo at his door. He told him of the attack and slaying of Labo. Tindal in return told Nau the women and children were crying because of the deaths of the other council members. It was immediately assumed Labo had decided to slay the members of the council for taking his son into custody on charges of sorcery. Frustration and anger gripped Nau and Tindal. They realized too late that Labo's earlier actions should have warned them to lock him up also, at least for the night, for the safety of the council and people of Nesal.

By now the whole village was awake with the street full of small talk. Tindal and Nau hurried back to Nau's house. Tindal wanted to see the slain Labo and Nau desired to check on his wife Amashai, his ten year-old son Hisum, and thirteen year-old daughter Misal.

Arriving back at Nau's house, Amashai had the door cracked open, but their children remained in their bedroom. Labo lay lifelessly on the ground, surrounded by those of the village. Cries from the other houses of the fallen council members lingered in the fog. Tindal asked all to move away so that he could see the body, so they did. Some moved to other homes and some simply stood back talking quietly.

Vandor knelt next to Kayla looking at the odd black-handled dagger that also drew Tindal's attention. "Where did you get that Nau?" Tindal questioned, having assumed it was Nau's own dagger with which he had slain Labo.

Nau informed them of the events as they took place, that this dagger was the weapon Labo had tried to slay him with and that it must also be the murder weapon of the fellow council members. Tindal agreed that it must be, but looked as though there were more to the dagger than simply being the weapon Labo had used.

"This is a *Gottlo* dagger. Legend claims this type of dagger is forged by the fire of a dragon and each is cursed with the power of *Ubils*. Although the handle is black, if you look closely you can see the raised symbol ⬥. Legend claims this symbol to be worn by the servants of *Darkness*, meaning the sworn enemies of the true *King*, King Salvare. There is no reason Labo should have had such a dagger unless..." Tindal looked around, ending abruptly what he was about to say.

Tindal paused then whispered where only Nau, Vandor, and Kayla could hear, "Legend declares it is the symbol of the *Wicked One*. It is the *mark* given to those that swear allegiance to the *Darkness*. Once the oath has been taken they are sealed with this *mark* upon their flesh and are his servants forever."

Kayla's eyes widened and mouth opened as if she were about to say something, but didn't.

"But Labo doesn't bare this *mark*," Nau pointed out.

Tindal looked at Labo's forehead, and true, there was no *mark*. Tindal knelt down beside Labo picking up Labo's left hand, searching it palm-to-back, and again he saw no *mark*. Reaching over, he lifted Labo's right hand and indeed saw the *mark* ☙ . Tindal looked up at the three.

"That *mark* wasn't there before," Vandor exclaimed surprised.

"Indeed, we would have seen it in our daily walk. Legend claims the evil spirits, the *Ubils*, have the ability to hide the *mark* that others may not see it. This would explain why he has such a dagger in his possession and why we never saw the *mark* before. Or, it could be that he has only recently received the *mark*," explained Tindal.

Kayla had been listening intently and asked, "So one may have this weapon and not have the *mark*? Can one be recovered from receiving the *mark*?"

Tindal began, "Legend says…," but was cut off abruptly by Vandor.

"Why do you keep saying, 'legend says' father? Are these things not contained in the *Book of Wisdom*?" Vandor fervently questioned. "Do you not believe they are much more than legend?"

Dismissing his son, for this was not the time or place for argument of such things, he answered Kayla, "Once a person has sworn allegiance and has taken the *mark* there is no known way to break the enchantment of the *Wicked One* or the evils spirits' control of that person. As for one having such a cursed weapon without first swearing allegiance and receiving the *mark*, I assume it is possible that one could have found or taken the blade from a slain *Gottlo*, but that would most likely not be the case, as we see here."

The discussion carried on and Vandor and Kayla turned the subject to Rayhold, since they had not seen him. They thought it odd that this was his father, yet he was nowhere to be found. There was talk of Rayhold and sorcery, through the idle chat of those in the village that night. Tindal explained what had transpired earlier in the evening, for it was neither Vandor nor Kayla who had given up Rayhold's secret. They were somewhat confused, for they believed they had been the only ones there to witness what had taken place. They silently questioned how Rayhold had escaped, and assumed his father had released him before he began to slay the council.

Vandor was grateful his father had been passed over by death this night.

Although frustrated by the council's and his father's actions, with the situation as it were, Vandor and Kayla refrained from mentioning their run-in with the *Gottlo* and seeing Rayhold use sorcery. They decided it would only complicate the matter, and Vandor was already upset that his father spoke of those things contained in the *Book of Wisdom* as if they were merely legend. Vandor also noticed how Kayla seemed to appear nervous and most inquisitive about the *mark* and the dagger.

Vandor began to ponder these things in his mind. He, Kayla, and Rayhold had met the *Gottlo* not that far from Nesal. Rayhold had used sorcery to slay the beast that attacked Kayla. They had sworn to not tell as of yet, but apparently another had seen and spoken it to the council. The council decided to apprehend Rayhold in the middle of the night. Rayhold was taken into custody but was now gone, and Labo's wife Sycress was no where to be found. Labo had slain members of the council with a dagger that was a weapon of the servants of *Darkness*. The dagger, Labo, and the *Gottlo* bore the same *mark* considered to be the *mark* of *Wicked One*.

Vandor considered these things and searched his thoughts for that which his grandfather, MaZak, had taught him through the years. MaZak had told him, that one day before the return of King Salvare, the *Darkness* would rise by the power of the *Wicked One* and encompass the land of Erde. He said there would be an increase of the things of *Darkness* and a decrease in knowledge and belief in the *Book of Wisdom*. In one week he had seen all this just in Nesal; for Rayhold had used sorcery, Labo had murdered using a cursed dagger, and his own father, Tindal, spoke as if the *Book of Wisdom* were merely legend. He feared his conclusion: The *Ekleipsis*.

# Insight and Understanding

*N*esal was in a state of unrest. Vandor walked alone with Kayla, as the village was still alive with the start of a new day soon breaking over the mountains. They held hands and quietly pondered many thoughts, not really speaking audibly to each other as they walked. Each was indulged deep in their own search for understanding of the recent events, and each took turns mumbling a few things out loud; trying to draw insight from the other, but it gave no comfort or enlightenment to either.

Vandor felt deep within himself that something of importance was happening. He wondered if this was the *Whisper* which the *Sealed* often spoke of. The writings within the *Book of Wisdom* bombarded his mind with those things spoken of by his grandfather. For a moment it all seemed clear that the *Ekleipsis* was indeed coming, but what were they to do?

Vandor suddenly turned to face Kayla and blurted out, "Kayla, I am going to Trachten to find grandfather."

They discussed the matter and Vandor knew he must not let his father know, for he would never allow such a travel for his son alone: especially now, with the deaths in Nesal. Kayla decided she would accompany him, and although Vandor objected to the idea, she demanded to do that which she would.

Realizing he could not persuade her to stay, he agreed they should travel together. They decided to pack light and to leave at once. They believed that while Nesal was still occupied with its current issues, they would have a better chance of leaving unnoticed.

As the first signs of light began to flourish, they were packed and slipping through the trees around the village upon their horses, ready to begin their journey. Never having been there before, Vandor could only go by the stories he had heard his grandfather speak of. He knew Trachten was due south west from Nesal, but not precisely the correct line to take. He knew it was beyond the Liban River, and decided they would ask villages along the way if need be.

They left Nesal and family behind as they headed to Trachten, speaking about what had recently taken place in their lives. It all still seemed as if it were but a dream, (oh, how they wished it were so!) but it was in fact every bit real. They picked up their speed and began to race to find MaZak. With the wind in their faces and the adrenalin passing from their mustangs to them as they rode, it freed their minds for a moment from worry. Smiles nearly broke their melancholy looks.

Coming near a shallow creek bed with flowing water, they decided to pause for a moment of refreshment. They dismounted their horses, leading them to the water. Vandor's bay-colored mustang, Korb, a magnificent male, carried a patch of white upon his forehead, a nearly black mane and tail, and dark brown socks. Kayla's palomino female, Dove, held a glorious golden coat, with a bright cream-colored mane and tail, with a small diamond white patch atop her darkened nose. Each had raised their companions from colts.

They tied the mustangs to an oak. Vandor knelt near the water, cupping handfuls and splashing them in his face. Rubbing his face and running his hands over his short brown hair to the back of his neck, he felt refreshed from the beating sun. Kayla massaged a generously damp cloth around her face and neck, rather than indulging in a full head shower as Vandor had seemed to think necessary.

Staring into the water, Vandor came to his senses and realized that Kayla's and his parents, along with others, were most likely searching the village and the nearby forest for them. He did decide to leave a short note to his mother, but he left it near her pillow where she would not quickly notice it, but would eventually find it. Kayla had not done the same for reasons she was about to share with Vandor.

"V." Kayla softly spoke, facing him as he rubbed the residue of water into his face. He looked at her as she continued. "I have seen one of those daggers before."

"What dagger Kayla?" Vandor gently questioned.

"The dagger that Rayhold's father had. The one with the symbol which your father claimed to be of the *Wicked One*, and carried by those *marked* as giving their allegiance to the *Darkness*," she replied.

Surprised, Vandor asked, "Where Kayla? Why didn't you tell me before?"

She explained, "Because it was my father's." A pause, "When I was a child, maybe six or seven, I was playing in my parents' room when I found a dagger in a drawer near my father's side of the bed. My mother came in to find me playing with it. She snatched the blade from my hands and gave me a good tongue lashing. She told me that it was not to be touched under any circumstances. She said I was to tell no one of the dagger and to not even mention to my father that I had ever seen it. Till this day I haven't.

"But I can still remember the look of that dagger and the symbol, for it intrigued me so even then. I fear now that my own father is but a *marked* man of the *Darkness*. Even your father said there is no hope for such, and I fear what that may mean for me, for us, and for Nesal."

Vandor wanted to comfort her, but with words he could not find. A deeper fear had arisen now. Had her father, Tebad, and Rayhold's father, Labo, worked together last night? Was her father also a murderer, or had Labo simply done that because they had taken Rayhold, and her father had just found the dagger? Was Nesal now in danger of Tebad also?

His thoughts were broken by a bright light shining into the corner of his eye from afar. He turned from Kayla to look in the direction from whence it came. He saw what appeared to be two children riding atop black ponies, but somehow they looked as short as children but older than such. He squinted and thought he recognized the sword one held. *That's my grandfather's sword!*

Vandor jumped up as if bitten by a serpent and dashed toward his mustang. He leaped upon Korb and pulled his sword from its sheath strapped to his saddle. Tapping the sides of Korb with his heals, Vandor moved toward the travelers. Kayla twisted up quickly, saddling Dove and trying to catch up to him. She hadn't a clue as to what had moved him, but she now saw those he was headed for across the creek. She thought it odd, but was too far behind to call to him.

As if gliding on air, Korb and Dove moved swiftly. In no time, Vandor confronted the two travelers. Vandor pulled Korb to a halt directly in front of them, and screamed, "Halt thieves," pointing his blade toward the male.

The male slowed his pony calling out, "Thieves we are not, but travelers to our homeland." The male moved the shiny sword he carried across his body and the female backed behind him.

Vandor could not get over how they appeared as children, but also as adults. He felt like someone was playing tricks with his mind. Their height and size showed the age of one nearly eight or nine, yet their face showed aged wisdom of one in their early thirties.

Kayla looked past Vandor and the male, taking notice of how the female watched over her male companion. The female had shoulder length blonde hair and soft features. Kayla could see the worry in the female's eyes, and noticed that she wore what appeared to be a long dress or skirt, which she pondered, *must make riding a pony difficult.*

Sitting tall on his mustang, which stood above the pony, Vandor used his height to his advantage. He stared down into the eyes of the male to examine him. Contrasted to his female companion's long blonde hair and smooth face, the male had short brown hair with a light beard. Vandor could clearly see these were not children, even though their size appeared to say so. Although small, the male showed no sign of shying away.

This close, Vandor could clearly see the engraving upon the blade of his grandfather's most prized position, *Reflection.* The male's hand was so small against the handle of the large sword. Fear and anger battled within Vandor's mind - Fear to ponder how such a small foe had come to bear his grandfather's sword and anger to slay him for whatever he had done to MaZak.

"How did you come about such a sword?" Vandor angrily questioned.

"It was given me by a man."

"Liar!" Vandor spit as he drew closer. The stress of all that had transpired had made Vandor more anxious and quick tempered than usual.

Tightening his grip to sturdy the blade, the male replied, "Ney, a man whom saved me wife and me life gave it to me."

Kayla and the female sat quietly upon their rides as the male egos battled it out. By now, Vandor and the male both feared the unknown of the other, and were confused by the situation itself. Neither would back down, nor did either wish to proceed to bloodshed.

Finally the female spoke, "The man died saving our lives in Trachten."

Vandor's instant pain would have been no different than if the male had driven MaZak's sword straight through his heart. The words pierced to the depth of his soul. Kayla's eyes widened, as she turned toward Vandor, shocked by the revelation. *It could not be*, the doubt wanted to rise within Vandor, but he somehow knew what the female spoke was true. How he wished it were not.

Vandor's firm straight stance slouched. The wind had been knocked from him. His eyes wanted to grieve for MaZak, but he would not allow them. Vandor still questioned who they were, and to what end their savior's death was caused in Trachten. He refused to allow himself to believe MaZak had perished, though the twisting and burning of his heart and stomach filled him with anguish.

Vandor's pain could not be hid upon his face. The male sensed Vandor's honesty and heartache, and decided to speak. "I am Wiltzer and this is me wife Damaris. We are dwarfs from Hozekan, where our people live. We were in Palvolin, the city in Trachten which be the place for the markets. Around midday the city was attacked by *Gottlos*. In the sky we saw that which we have never seen before; a dark creature able to spit fire from his jaws which made an awful sound indeed. It could fly like a bird, but was larger than any we have ever known, having not feathers, but plates of armor.

"The people were running everywhere trying to escape the *Gottlos*, this flying creature, and the fire burning all around us. Us being shorter than most, we were having trouble avoiding the stampede of the crowd. This older man came through the midst of the people and took hold of me wife and me. He carried us away from the people and the suffocating smoke.

"This brute beast with wings landed near us and we were afraid. Smoke flowed from his large nostrils, and his emerald eyes seemed to draw one in as they sparkled. The beast stood taller that the trees in Hozekan and each scale looked the size of a wagon wheel or greater. It had horns like an ox and a squeal like an eagle, almost the mannerisms of a man with the fierceness of a lion.

"Riding the beast, which the man called *Rubicund*, was a ghostly figure that appeared as death itself, but spoke as a man. He wore a dark cloak and we could not see his face. He called out to the man as if he knew him. The figure screamed to the man that the *King* had betrayed everyone here in Erde and was dead. I am not sure what or who he spoke of, but he said that this *King* would never return. He told the man to submit to the service of Jagare and he might be allowed to live.

"The man seemed surprisingly confident that the cloaked figure was wrong and showed pure bravery in the face of such a beast. He threw me this blade, which he had held, and told me to leave Trachten immediately and warn my countrymen in Hozekan. How he knew of Hozekan, I know not, but he claimed it was of the utmost importance that we survive to tell others of something called the *Ekleipsis*. There was no time to ask questions, so I trusted the man that saved our lives.

"We knew we were too short to escape quickly, for our small legs do not allow us to stride as far and fast as you tall ones," he said with a grin.

"We found a hiding place to wait for darkness. The *Gottlos* have taken over at least Palvolin and have set up an image of this same flying beast, along with a man which stands before it. We heard them speak of leading the people of Erde there, to swear allegiance to some Jagare and the beast, or to be slain. It took us two days to silently escape, by maneuvering around the large army there.

"It took all our monies, after escaping Trachten, to purchase these two ponies. We are on our way to our home in Hozekan to warn our people. To be honest, of what, we are not sure. For this *Ekleipsis* still seems quite confusing to us."

Something inside Vandor urged him to trust this male dwarf named Wiltzer, although he could not recall ever hearing the term dwarf being used or spoken of before. He had listened intently and noticed Wiltzer had left out an important detail he wished know, "What happened to this man that gave you the sword?"

"The man..." A sad look seemed to show in the dwarf's eyes, "The man stood his ground. He spoke to the dark figure and claimed that if he would allow me wife and me to go free for the present, he would submit to this Jagare and *Rubicund*'s control. This *Rubicund* must be the name of the flying beast but I am not sure of it, and I am unclear as to who this Jagare is.

"Permission was granted with a grin, but most likely the figure was sure we would die there by the hand of one of the *Gottlos*. Actually we have never heard or seen one of these so-called *Gottlos*, but that is what people were yelling, so I assume that is what they are. Ugly creatures indeed; almost like a man, but more like a beast themselves and equally taller than a man than we are shorter.

"Me wife and me ran with all our might toward an area that seemed the easiest place to hide, with the least amount of people. I glanced over my shoulder as I saw the flying beast lower its head to draw the dark figure closer to the man. The man stood there unmoving. As the dark figure drew near, I saw the man pull something from around his back, from under his shirt, and throw it toward the figure. It looked like a dagger, which stuck in the figure's shoulder as it screamed out. The man turned to run, but the breath of the flying beast engulfed him in flames. The flying beast and its rider then flew away as those *Gottlos* continued to kill and destroy everything in sight.

"Oh, we also heard the name or word *Ubils*, but I don't believe saw who or what they were. Have you ever heard of any of this which I have spoken to you?"

All eyes were on Vandor to see what he would do or say. "Was there another man with this man that gave you the sword," he said, speaking of Dartego.

"No other man. This man was alone when we saw him, but Palvolin was full of people running and fighting these *Gottlos*, so there could have been another we did not see."

Vandor lowered his sword. Wiltzer did the same. Not that there was complete understanding, but a degree of honesty was felt between the two. A willingness to accept what the other had said and to trust, at least momentarily the character of one another, they decided to dismount and converse for awhile.

Kayla and Damaris, the dwarf's wife, found it most comforting, now that it appeared there would be no bloodshed today. Both felt they had recently seen enough.

Vandor sat amidst the soft clover, resting his back against a tree and Kayla rested near him. Wiltzer sat against a wide stump with enough room for his wife Damaris to join him with her hand upon his thigh. Both Vandor and Wiltzer sat with their blades unsheathed at close arms length. All were quiet for a moment.

"What were you doing in Trachten?" questioned Vandor.

"Our people live in Hozekan, south east from here. Until most recently, we were forbidden to venture from Hozekan into the inner regions of Erde. Our last emperor, Emperor Oviss, which was one of the first of our kind, forbid any dwarf access to Erde outside of the Valtava Forest, which surrounds and hides Hozekan. He swore that any dwarf found past the Valtava Forest would be forever cutoff from the dwarfs, and if they returned, they would die the death. (Meaning death by burning, with their ashes spread outside of Hozekan, to be forever cutoff from their people.)

"He recently died leaving his son, now Emperor Penuh Harap, to reign in his stead. Although Emperor Oviss was a wise dwarf, he was most afraid of what lay outside of the Valtava Forest, within the central parts of Erde. Emperor Penuh Harap is less fearful than his father, but from what I have seen most recently, there may be warrant to Emperor Oviss' fears.

"Since Emperor Penuh Harap has overridden his father's law of travel outside of Hozekan, most have not been brave enough to venture outside of our commune. Me wife had heard through idle chat that far west from Hozekan there was a city called Trachten, that held markets twice a year, where all were allowed to come and sell their items. There are many precious and beautiful stones in Hozekan, so me wife and me decided to travel the great distance this time to see if we could sell our stones, and also to see that which we have never been allowed to," Wiltzer explained.

"Why were you not allowed to leave your city?" Kayla questioned.

"Legend claims, as did Emperor Oviss attest, along with the council that once lived, that many moons ago the dwarfs were but a few among many giants, which I now wonder if he meant merely your kind. Yet now, I further wonder if we are really different kinds at all, for there seems to be hardly much diversity but in size.

"They told us of a wicked giant and a righteous giant, and that the wicked giant had slain the righteous giant. We were told that the wicked giant had power over many evil creatures and spirits that roamed freely in Erde, because the righteous giant no longer lived to battle them. Which I now assume must be these *Gottlos* and *Ubils* I heard the people speak of.

"They insisted that Emperor Oviss had gathered all of the dwarfs that he could find, and traveled secretly through the Valtava Forest into what is now known as Hozekan. He immediately passed the law that none were to venture past the Valtava Forest into the nether parts of Erde. The lands outside of Hozekan were now seen as an evil place of wickedness. For fear that it would lead them to override us in Hozekan if we were found out, it was simply determined as forbidden to leave.

"When Emperor Penuh Harap took leadership, he sent spies into Erde, which reported back to him. Upon testimony of the spies, the council claimed that Erde was not as bad as his father had claimed. Not doubting his father, Penuh Harap assumed the wickedness that Oviss had spoken of had now past, but it appears that it has not.

"Further teaching also told of the righteous king one day returning to cleanse the land of Erde of all wickedness, and all those that oppose good. Although no righteous king had been found by any of the spies, Emperor Penuh Harap assumed this king may have yet returned and was the reason for the spies not seeing the total wickedness his father had spoken of in Erde."

"Pardon me for asking, but why then did you call us thieves and what interest do you have in this here sword and the man which gave it to me?"

Vandor found what this dwarf had said most interesting, as it was similar to what had actually taken place in Erde, but from a perspective of people which were hidden from the actual events as they took place. Vandor began to expound, "My name is Vandor and this is Kayla. The sword which you bear is my grandfather's most prized work. His name is MaZak and the name of that sword he called *Reflection*. We were on our way to Trachten to meet him when I saw the glimmer of his blade that you carry."

"We are sorry to be the bearer of your loss, but we are most grateful for him saving our lives," Damaris softly added.

Vandor continued to push the idea of the death of his grandfather further from his mind. By all accounts, this perished soul could have been Dartego, which would have hurt almost as much as if it were his grandfather, or yet another person who his grandfather had only lent his sword to in the battle. "I believe your story is very similar to the truth of what has actually happened here in Erde."

Vandor could see the dwarf's face wrinkle as if to say, *You are calling Emperor Oviss a liar*, so he quickly added, "I mean no disrespect, but my grandfather has lived quite sometime through the struggles of the land of Erde, and there are many which bear record of the same accounts. I am by no means saying that your Emperor Oviss' stories are made up, but they appear to be more legend and parable based on the truth of how he saw or heard it."

Vandor saw a relaxed look from Wiltzer, so he continued. Vandor told of King Salvare, of his *Book of Wisdom*, and how he loved and helped the people of Erde. He ensured Wiltzer that this must be the righteous king that his emperor had spoken of. And this righteous king had established a voluntary group called the *Sealed* to follow his lead, proclaim his truth, and serve in the land of Erde with a godly standard of honesty and love for things that are right.

He then told him of Judarius and how he had betrayed King Salvare and had slain him. He claimed that, even though Judarius was never a true king, this must have been the wicked king the dwarf emperor had proclaimed. He explained how Judarius and his seed, the wicked Galtare and Jagare which followed, had warriors such as *Gottlos*, evil creatures which some claimed used to be men, and *Ubils*, evil spirits which are able to persecute men unseen.

Vandor went on the explain that Judarius had moved the land of Erde into dark times, but at his death his son Galtare had pushed Erde into the *Dark Ages* trying to remove all remembrance of King Salvare, his *Book of Wisdom*, and all that was good. He further spoke of the failing years of Galtare, whereby the *Sealed* were reborn and Kirche was established in Signum, for the purpose of bringing the light back to the land of Erde.

He told of the death of Galtare and the rise of his son Jagare, which desired to tear down what the *Sealed* had built in Signum, while his father Galtare lay sick or mentally disabled. He entailed that an unknown person had struck a deadly blow to Jagare's head with an arrow, which had given this occasion of somewhat rest in Erde. He assumed the dwarfs must have missed this *Great Awakening* while they hid in Hozekan.

Vandor gave regard to the telling of the *pale* Piradad, who had ridden a dragon name *Rubicund* into *Oscuridad* (explaining this must be the flying beast which they saw in Trachten), the kingdom of *Darkness* past the *Shadow Lands* on the edge of Erde. This *Rubicund*, which most had never seen but only heard of, from the land down under called Kriminala Pasaule, apparently had the power to revive Jagare from his deadly wound, but Jagare had yet to be seen or heard from.

Most importantly, he spoke of the power of King Salvare's father, King Allmachtig, who dwelled in the far kingdom of Himmel, and of how this mighty king had the power to raise his martyred son from the grave. He told of how King Salvare had left to go to his father's kingdom, but had promised to return with an army to defeat all that is wicked in the land of Erde. That this King

Salvare had promised to return, bringing with him a kingdom of rest called *Scimerian* to his children, meaning those who love and serve him.

Vandor continued his story to Wiltzer and Damaris, up until the present dismay of things. He told of the *mark* which he had seen upon the *Gottlos*, on Labo, and the dagger which Labo had used. Though he refrained from speaking of Kayla's father, who they feared also had one such dagger and could possibility bear the *mark* of the *Wicked One*. He explained how it all made sense now - the *mark*, the attack in Trachten, the graven image, and the army of *Gottlos* and *Ubils* which Wiltzer had claimed to see.

Vandor explained that all the signs pointed to what Judarius had claimed as the *Ekleipsis*. This would be the day in which all good would be taken from the land of Erde, as the *Darkness* would rule, slaying all who opposed it. Yet he was confident in King Salvare and his *Book of Wisdom*, whereby it was written that he indeed would return and save his people from the *Wicked One*.

When Vandor was finished, the dwarfs sat silently as if soaking in all of that which he spoken. He had tried to share that which the *Book of Wisdom* and his grandfather had often spoken of. Placing it into the context with what he believed concerning the recent events he had experienced, added with those Wiltzer had mentioned. He feared the worst, but refused to give doubt the advantage over his belief that indeed, King Salvare would return before Jagare would be able to destroy all that was good in Erde.


"You have persuaded me to believe that which you say. Knowing that which Emperor Oviss spoke, and trusting what you have told us here to be true, indeed the stories tell of the same evil that seems to be once again taking hold of the land of Erde. I only fear that now since we have the freedom to venture from the Hozekan, we may no longer be safe from it," Wiltzer acknowledged. "How can I know more of this King Salvare and his book?"

Vandor stood, leaving his sword, and walked to his saddle bags upon Korb. From the bag he pulled a book. He walked back and held it out to

Wiltzer. Wiltzer took the book with both hands. Its cover was made of black leather, somewhat faded, with tattered edges. The pages looked dirty and used. The inscription was worn, but the title could still be faintly seen, King Salvare's *Book of Wisdom*. Wiltzer took the book, holding it in awe; it was a history and a revelation of which he had never read.

Wiltzer offered Vandor back his grandfather's sword, but Vandor asked him to keep it. "Regardless of the circumstances, if indeed my grandfather gave you the sword, then it is yours. It may also serve as proof to what you must tell your emperor and people regarding the coming threat to all of the land of Erde."

Wiltzer acknowledged Vandor's words and agreed. Wiltzer stood, as did Damaris, and spoke. "We must be on our way to Hozekan to warn our people and share this book with Emperor Penuh Harap. I will share with him the story of the man and his sword, and your story of Erde and what you have recently seen. There is much preparation that must be made and I fear we have no time."

Wiltzer paused, taking a glance at Kayla, then returning to Vandor, "Where are you two headed?"

"We were on our way to see my grandfather in Trachten. I feel I must continue that direction to see if indeed it was he of whom you speak, or if by chance it was his friend Dartego, or yet even another," Vandor answered.

"Dear Sir, Trachten is no place for the likes of you two. It is crawling with detestable creatures than cannot be numbered. I am fearful that even the flying beast frequently returns there. If you are captured you will surely be tortured and lose your life for naught. Do you not fear death? If by chance your grandfather or friend were yet alive in Trachten, they most likely would have perished by now," Wiltzer begged.

"I shall only pass along the outskirts of Trachten, and turn upward toward Signum where the *Sealed* dwell in Kirche. It may be that my grandfather and or Dartego were able to escape the attack, and make it there to warn them.

If they have not, then I shall share the news of Trachten and that of Nesal to the Auctoritas, Ciafus. The *Sealed* will be our only chance if we are to survive an attack of an army, which may have only been growing while sitting in silence. There are also some questions we have for them there," Vandor told.

"I must say I fear for your safety, but we have no time to stand here arguing over what must be done. May the Creator grant you protection against these wicked souls. I pray we shall meet again as friends, and that our people may know one another. Perhaps at the return of this righteous king of yours, it may be so," Wiltzer replied.

Within such a short time, seemingly foes became friends, with a common desire: to save the souls of Erde (and Hozekan) from the *Darkness*. Wiltzer and Damaris headed toward Hozekan upon their ponies, with Vandor and Kayla riding their mustangs toward Trachten. Over their shoulders, they wished each other well upon their journeys.

# Meeting of the Gibborims

*I*t was a chilly, dark night that the *Gibborims* met under the full moon inside the halls of the castle of their eldest brother, Jagare, the totalitarian over them and their surrounding lesser kingdoms, upon Mount Dauthus in *Oscuridad*. It was not so much that they submitted to his rule full-heartedly with gladness, but more so by an instilled fear from childhood. His dominance and demand for prominence had been since birth.

§ § § §

Born of the wives and concubines of Galtare were these. Jagare was born of Galtare's first wife Elinora, which Galtare slew in anger. Essen, his second wife, bore him Desgosto, yet died of consumption when he was but three. Of the concubine Mayaton were born the twins Baitrs and Begeren. Most beloved, she also bore him Zolba his youngest child of eleven. Gniew, his fifth child, coming after Begeren, was born of the concubine Salena. Taken against her will from Nikoden, she bore him in disgust, so Galtare gave her over to his *Gottlos* as a prostitute. Karlami, yet another concubine, bore him his second twins Hatan and Himo. His third wife Vira bore him yet a third set of twins, Abejoti and Ahnews, along with his tenth child before Zolba, named Pyktis.

Eldest, Jagare was a most hateful child. Each of the brothers could clearly remember the times that Jagare had caused them pain and sufferings for his mere pleasure. Most were emotional scars tucked deep away, which made them grow angered and terrible toward all creatures. But there were also those which bore the physical marks of their brother's torments upon them; such as Pyktis's missing little finger upon his left hand, and the scar across the cheek of Gniew. Fear of Jagare caused them to lash out happily upon all else that was, merely venting their frustrations which drew from another source.

A council of hatred this was; hatred for all that is right and good in the sight of the people of Erde, and their precious missed King Salvare. Jagare was well-voiced in playing this hatred of all, which he himself had caused to form within the bosoms of his kin, to his favor and desires. His brothers were easily persuaded and he looked at them as evolutionary lesser, as delinquent handicaps. To him, they were none other than obedient fools, no greater than the *Gottlos* they command, yet he told them not. Jagare had always played their egos and madness against them, to easily persuade their allegiance to his causes.

§    §    §    §

This night was an important night, as the *Gibborims* arrived at Jagare's castle, upon Mount Dauthus, to discuss the ideals of their brother. Enormous stone walls encompassed the banquet hall, which was large enough to hold at least a hundred mighty men. Centered in the room were a row of two solid twelve-foot wooden tables covered in wild game and domestic meats, fresh and preserved vegetables and fruits, variety of breads, with bitter wines and strong drink to fill their rages. A splendid feast had been prepared, with cushioned chairs and golden steins awaiting their arrival.

*Oscuridad* being home to Jagare and all of his kin, they were soon gathered together at the center, Mount Dauthus. Hatan, Baitrs, Gniew, Pyktis, and Zolba from the north arrived first. Soon to follow were Desgosto, Abejoti,

Himo, Ahnews, and Begeren from the south. They merely awaited Jagare's presence.

These mighty men towered above the normal people of Erde, in height and depth. Some said they must be possessed by *Ubils*, the evil spirits, giving them supernatural ability. Some went as far back as Judarius, claiming he was the offspring of a fallen *Malaikat* (a spiritual messenger of the Great Creator, God, whereby a *Malaikat* became an *Ubil* when fallen from obedience). They believed his mother Bailite, who claimed she was overtaken by an invisible oppressor, brought forth from her womb the seed of mankind and *Malaikat* (*Ubil*) unto all his kindred till this day. Yet there were also those that gave no credence to supernatural ideas, saying it was merely evolutionary natural selection at work. By whatever means, they were feared indeed, and were known throughout Erde as the *Gibborims*.

From the time of the piercing of Jagare, which brought him beyond the veil of death, only to be returned to the living by the power of *Rubicund*, that dragon from Kriminala Pasaule, with the *pale* Piradad, they have remained still, whereby the land of Erde was able to rest as it were until now. They have grown weary of rest, and desire to fill their evil lusts. They waited only for the permission of their eldest brother Jagare, to delight themselves in the acting out their vain imaginations upon the people of Erde.

Dressed in a mixture of fur, leather, and metal armory, there were helmets, swords, daggers, shields and the like, hung on the walls, worn on their sides, and laid around the room as they waited in anticipation. They dared not disrespect Jagare by tasting that which lay upon the tables, while he was not among them. They knew he was merely testing them, and by no means did any wish to endure his wrath.

The room was filled with derogatory talk of the vilest things. Talk of kidnapping children for slaves, taking young maidens as concubines, slaying the old and crippling the young men and most hated, what to do about Kirche in Signum, where the *Sealed* were. Once in their grasp, they believed all light would vanish in their grip. They did not realize they were merely pawns in the hands of their brother Jagare, the *Wicked One*, and if successful in their banishment of light, what then should they have? For in *Darkness*, what then could be seen?

A cracking sound came as the door opened. All twisted to the entrance, and quieted their grumblings of violence. Frozen as statues, refusing to blink, they expected their brother to appear. Piradad entered the room, allowing the brothers' stony hearts to briefly relax.

Piradad was but a small skeleton to these brothers, yet they listened to him speak, for they knew Jagare must be most near. "Dear brothers of Jagare, ye *Gibborims* take heed. The time of your wait is now over. Now enters the days of the fulfillment of your lusts by lord Jagare Morte. Him shall you serve. Him shall you obey, that your desires may be fulfilled throughout all of Erde."

A voice of cheers, with the pounding of fists upon the tables, the *Gibborims'* blood thirsty souls united. Then there was silence as Jagare entered the room, with Piradad stepping aside to give way.

"My dear brothers," Jagare called, walking toward the tables, opening his arms as if to embrace them. "I have long awaited this reunion of the children of our father Galtare, seed of our grandfather Judarius, son of the chosen Bailite and the power of *Darkness*."

Pausing, he reached his arms toward the tables, "Sit my brothers, tonight we meet for the purpose of a new order for the land of Erde."

As they took their seats, he moved to his place at the head of the tables, facing the direction of the entrance from whence he had entered.

While the brothers sat, Jagare stood, at the forefront. "My brothers, I am Jagare the eldest son of Galtare, son of Judarius, heir of the *Darkness*, slayer of the old king of Erde, and am hereby worthy to be called King of all of Erde!"

His eyes peered from side to side, taking notice of his brothers' countenances as he continued. "To this end have I called you here. To this end will I rise to power and slay all who oppose me. I shall be their master, and I shall be a god unto them. Ye shall be my horsemen as all in Erde bow the knee to King Jagare!"

No cheers, only silence, Jagare asked, "What say ye?"

The stillness at the tables was broken by Desgosto, the second born. He stood to face Jagare, equal in height but slightly broader. Talking with his hands, the tight brass wrist bands caused his forearms to bulge. "Brother Jagare, what is this that you speak? Why cannot Erde be broken into eleven kingdoms for us all?"

A few mumbled comments of agreement came from the twins, Baitrs and Begeren, but all else were quiet.

"What right do you have for all of Erde that we do not all share, being all sons of Galtare and sons of Judarius?" Desgosto asked, making eye contact with all of his brothers, and then returning to Jagare.

"Dear Desgosto, my brother. What have you done worthy of an inheritance of Erde? Have you not sat in your castle as a spoiled child doing nothing? Did you avenge the attempt on my life? You have but lived off of my power and might, and there shall you remain," calmly but firm, replied Jagare.

Pointing fiercely at Jagare, Desgosto claimed, "A lie! I have asked you for nothing and shall never ask you for anything! You were yet vile to us as children, and here remain one that thinks he is above all." Desgosto's voice and blood pressure rose, as the thoughts of childhood and the years of hate of his brother Jagare, bottled up inside, began to release themselves all at once. "We have allowed you the rule you hold, but I am afraid of you no more. You are but a brute beast!"

Tension built in the room. The brothers held still with silence, glancing back and forth between the stares of Jagare and Desgosto. This was not the first argument they had seen between brothers, but it had been many years since one had been brave enough to challenge Jagare directly. It was by this means that Gniew bore the scar on his face from the angered slash of a blackened dagger from Jagare, and the loss of Pyktis's little finger by the same dagger and fierceness of Jagare. These two remained silent, Gniew subconsciously touched his scar, and Pyktis looked down at his left hand.

"Dear Desgosto, do you despise that which you have been given? Do you believe you merit more? By chance, do you hold the notion that you should be King of Erde with me and your brothers as your servants?" questioned Jagare.

"Your words are meaningless Jagare, which you always used to your gain. You have given me nothing, but our father Galtare has given us all lordship over portions of *Oscuridad*, with thine being the greatest. You have given us nothing, but desire to take all of Erde to yourself and even now to enslave your own brothers to be but your mere servants," Desgosto answered.

Jagare searched the eyes of his brothers, "Be this true dear brothers? Does your allegiance lie with Desgosto and his railings against me? Or, do you wish to bond with me this day, to take all of Erde under one kingdom, whereby you shall be as mighty men over the mere mortals of this land?!"

A few shouts of agreement were broken by the words of Desgosto once more. "Ask them not Jagare, for it is I who condemn you as a mad man. You have yet to be proven worthy to be king, for it was you who fell in battle by the arrow of the unknown, which could be a mere peasant girl."

Jagare recoiled like a viper. "Hold your tongue Desgosto, lest it be cut from your jaws this very day. I have power and means at my disposal you know not of. Do not be as the foolish, who think they are able to speak ill of King Jagare and live."

Desgosto's anger moved him to further taunt his brother. "I defy this King Jagare that is not, but remains yet a wounded mind babbling tyrant."

Pulling his sword from the sheath along his side, Desgosto spewed, "By all means I challenge you, dear Jagare, for your portion of *Oscuridad* and all of Erde."

Gasps, even from these giants among men, could be heard. The seriousness of this had surpassed the rivalry of brothers, and had moved to battle of supremacy among men. Pride and ego had pushed all essence of wisdom away, leaving only the desire to have that which the other wanted: the lust for power, the desire to be lord over all.

Many men have gone forth with clouded judgment, by the urges of their lustful hearts, only to end in despair.

Lifting his arm, as if swatting a fly with the back of his hand, Jagare exclaimed, "Let it be as you have said dear Desgosto, I shall miss you."

As Jagare's wrist popped upward, Desgosto flew backwards, knocking over the chair and slamming against the wall.

Jagare moved around the tables toward Desgosto, "Fear me brothers, but do not defy me. Ye shall receive that which you are due. Am I not able to give that which I please?"

No one said a word as Desgosto appeared to be penned against the wall. He struggled for breath, as if something was caught in his throat. He fought the claustrophobic feeling of not being able to move, completely confined to the position of the wall. Sweat began to pour from his face as his inner being seemed to pull and tear itself from his flesh, as he tried to break free of Jagare's grip. Grunts could be made out, but his mouth refused to obey the commands of his jumbled mind. Fear and hatred of Jagare drove Desgosto mad as he could not act upon either. The *Ubils* within him cried out in torment, further adding to Desgosto's madness.

Jagare paced within five feet of Desgosto, staring him in the eyes. "Dear brother Desgosto, I asked you here for your allegiance, but I feel as though I no longer need it. You desire not to serve me, so I shall give you over to the fires of the *Dragon*. They shall not consume you, but torment you far beyond time. Ye shall curse my name and I shall not hear it, ye shall beg for mercy and I shall not give it. Fear it, for it waits for you! I give you over to the living flames of hell!"

Instantly Desgosto's entire being ignited with invisible flames, as human combustion which could not be seen with the naked eye. The flames were not visible, but the heat could be felt and the burning flesh could be smelled. The brothers watched Desgosto, and all that he bore, melt before their eyes, as he screamed out in pain. He begged for mercy where there was none, his body became charred and lifeless. It was a grotesque sight, far more horrific than one being burned alive, when much of the sight is hidden by the flames. These hidden flames, which consumed Desgosto before their very eyes, bore record to the *Gibborims*, no mercy laid in the heart of their brother Jagare.

Jagare turned to the brothers, "Any other objections dear brothers, or shall we proceed to the feast?"

# Hozekan Warning

*T*he dwarfs, Wiltzer and his wife Damaris, wasted no time in their journey back to Hozekan. Their black ponies did not move as swiftly as mustangs or stallions, but they pressed on to the timbers of the Valtava Forrest full gust. With new knowledge, considering it but a fuller understanding of what was, what is, and what is to come, with book in hand, Wiltzer wished that they were already speaking to Emperor Penuh Harap. Questions of how to present his case, and worries of whether the emperor and the council would heed his warning filled his mind, as the wind blew hard against his beard.

Mixed with the fears for his people, he could not hide the thoughts of worry he had for young Vandor and his companion, Kayla. He had seen the Land of the *Seekers*, the death and destruction that lay within, and the evil that now dwelled there. He was most sure the young boy would not find his grandfather among the living, and how would they escape the grasps of the *Gottlos*, if by chance, they were caught? Turning back, he could possibly persuade the young pair to refrain from Trachten altogether, but by doing so, would it not leave his own people awaiting the coming *Ekleipsis* without warning? Should he save the two over the lives of an entire race? He knew his duty was to warn the hidden people of Hozekan, so he prayed no ill would befall the young couple.

Arriving at the Valtava Forrest, the entrance into Hozekan, the hearts of the two dwarfs found both comfort and eagerness to share their new knowledge with the others. Met by Paktil and Qwen, the *watchmen*, at the forefront of Hozekan, they were the first alarm to the people. It was somewhat easy for a dwarf to recognize a dwarf, and very few men had found their way into these parts, so Paktil and Qwen came forth from their hiding places to welcome Wiltzer and Damaris home. Showing their dwarf insignia rings was merely formality more than anything. Each dwarf was given such a ring, made of white gold, to be worn on their left ring finger, when they reached the age of sixteen (the age of adulthood), with the blackened symbol:

For fear of alarming all the souls of Hozekan, Wiltzer and Damaris decided to hold their tongues till they were able to be granted company with Emperor Penuh Harap. Informing the *watchmen* that they had something of great importance to tell the emperor, Paktil left them, making his way to the palace in the center of Hozekan, to inform the council. Qwen questioned Wiltzer as to the book and sword he carried, but Wiltzer replied that the emperor must hear of it first. Walking past the enormous *sikwayi*[f], bearing a large carving of the dwarf emblem, matching that of the rings, Qwen did not question them further.

Standing in front of the palace, Wiltzer took a moment to enjoy the craftsmanship his father had once taken part in. Its height was almost equal to that of the trees of the Valtava Forest, which were the tallest in all of Erde, and its length equally long. It was completely made from the thick *sikwayi* timbers of

---

[f] the largest trees in Erde, found only in the Valtava Forest, which surround Hozekan

the forest. Handcrafted engravings of the late Emperor Oviss, along with dwarf symbols and writings covered it beautifully. Completely recoated yearly by hand with a special sap mixture made from the *mahla*[f] trees, the palace shined brightly with the rays of the sun. So much so, that when the glaze was fresh, one must almost squint as they walk by, and the glow from the light of the moon upon it could be seen amidst the middle of the village at night.

Once the council was gathered, Paktil came forth from the palace entrance, informing Wiltzer and Damaris that the emperor and council would see *him* now. Wiltzer could feel his stomach tighten and looked at his wife. Damaris gave her husband a silent gaze of confidence and encouragement, with a look of love in her eyes. Wiltzer took a deep breath, and followed Paktil into the palace, to the council chamber room. This was where decisions were made. To the rise or fall of Hozekan, Wiltzer was there to request such an action.

Paktil walked Wiltzer and Damaris up to the large wooden doors of the council chamber room. The dwarf emblem was boldly engraved upon the door, with the following words:

**"Though short in stature, all things are within our reach."**

Paktil made motion to Damaris that she could sit in either of the crimson cushioned chairs, marvelously handcrafted from *stejar*[f] wood, set on each side of the chamber entrance. Damaris took a seat, giving her husband a passionate wink with a smile.

Paktil opened the chamber door revealing the six members sitting on the far side of the table. The table had the appearance of an enormous, polished *sikwayi* tree trunk, cut squarely across the top, twelve foot long. Smoothly rounded underneath, it stood on four legs, each the size of a dwarf's thigh. Among the council, from Wiltzer's left to right, were as follows: Cohart, Fiken, Guesald, Imbol, Wedgmark, and the eldest, Falinn Viden. Wiltzer knew of them all, but not personally.

Emperor Penuh Harap sat behind the council, upon a slightly elevated platform, in a chair made of thick *sikwayi*. Deep purple shawls, with gold trim and tassels, flowed from each arm of the chair, and covered the chair from head to foot. They matched the emperor's purple royal robe, lined with three inch gold strips, around the hems and down the front and back, flowing from the ring around the collar. He also wore a golden crown, handed down from Emperor Oviss, which had been said to have come from Signum in Erde.

A single chair, matching the two at the entrance, awaited Wiltzer across the table from the onlookers. It was a far twenty feet to walk. As he stepped, he could hear the light sounds of the creaking wood beneath his feet. He stopped before the chair, bowed and waited for the emperor to speak.

"Welcome Wiltzer," warmed Emperor Penuh Harap. "Paktil has told us that you have certain information that you feel is most important to the council and I. Please be seated and share with us this news," the emperor spoke softly with open arms.

Wiltzer placed the sword, now wrapped in cloth, and the book on the table in front of the seat he took. Pulling closer to the table, a slight skidding

[f] a type of oak, only found around Hozekan

sound was made, but no one seemed to notice. All eyes were fixed upon his countenance and awaiting his words.

Wiltzer began, softly speaking, "Dear emperor and Council of Hozekan, please pardon me tongue, for I am not much of a speaker." Not a face changed emotion, so he continued, "Me wife and I have been to Trachten, and I fear what we have seen."

Wiltzer continued to tell them of the things which he beheld in Trachten and his fear that Hozekan may no longer be safe. They all listened intently to what was said. Wiltzer stopped short of telling of Vandor, Kayla, and the book he now had, for he wondered if any believed him thus far.

Cohart, the youngest and newest member, was first to reply. "Dear Wiltzer, have you yet another witness to these accounts? For the law states 'let therefore the truth of any matter be established by the observance of two or more witnesses. Else, let it be examined by the council that it may be judged righteously.'"

In Hozekan, a female dwarf's word was not regarded as highly as a male's, even in some cases of defense and prosecution. Thus was why Wiltzer had entered, and his wife, Damaris, waited for him seated without. Since his inheritance of emperor, Penuh Harap had thought to change such a law, but he knew such matters must be handled delicately. One could not change all things overnight, and expect to remain well-liked and respected. For this cause, he intended to have Damaris speak if need be, after the council had heard Wiltzer.

"Cohart. Bid this dwarf his time, for it is the council in which he has brought forth this matter," claimed the emperor.

"Yes, dear council, me wife is a witness, and I have these two items which bare record of that which I tell." Wiltzer unclothed the sword, "This sword bares record of the man who gave himself to free me wife and me from the flying beast and evil doers in Trachten. I have reason to believe his name was MaZak, also known as *The Bladesman*, as he served as one of the *Sealed* for many years under a righteous King Salvare, which was slain, yet lives again, and of whom those in Erde await his return, that the *Darkness* may be cast out forever."

"How can you be certain of such? Who is this King Salvare of which you speak? We have never heard one of such name, nor do we know of any such righteous king, but that one whom was slain in the history before Hozekan," claimed Wedgmark.

"Can you not see, as I have told you the truth, in what I have spoken, it but tells of the same story of that which Emperor Oviss and the council had written in the *Legend of Pre-Hozekan*?" pleaded Wiltzer.

"That could be any man's sword, and this King Salvare, of which you speak, could be but one that wishes to claim all of Erde as his own, including our beloved Hozekan," added Guesald.

"Indeed, I trust your words that wickedness now seems to dwell in Trachten, of which my father often spoke, and thus forbid us from leaving Hozekan. Have we been too eager to suppose that which the fathers spoke of was mere legend, and that there is no real evil in Erde to be warned of?" The emperor paused for a moment, as his eyes drifted into thought, "How have you come to know so much, and seem so sure that the legend of which the fathers spoke contains more truth than we were given?"

"Dear emperor, I met this young man upon my return to Hozekan, who knew the bearer of this sword as his grandfather MaZak, and he spoke of the stories of which his grandfather had lived," Wiltzer answered.

"Yet, how can you trust this man that you have never met before?" questioned Guesald.

"For those things of which he spoke were similar to those which were of Emperor Oviss' own words, and a great amount of truth is contained within the pages of this book he gave me." Wiltzer took the book, which had been laying face down upon the table, lifted it up, with the title facing toward council. "This is King Salvare's *Book of Wisdom*. It holds further revelation of that which we dwarfs have in the *Legend of Pre-Hozekan*."

Wedgmark stiffened, as he claimed, "Have you gone mad? Dare you say that this book, of these unknown men, holds more truth, or bares further record than that which has come from the pure mouths of our fathers."

A warm rush came over Wiltzer's face. This was not going as he had hoped. He blamed himself. If he could have only conveyed into words that which he knew in his mind, and felt in his heart to be true. Wiltzer knew that which he spoke would mean the life or death of the souls in Hozekan, but felt he had only caused the council to doubt and become disgusted with his thoughts. Maybe if his wife had been the one to speak. Maybe he should have asked Vandor and Kayla to accompany him back to Hozekan, for Vandor's words had been so clear to understand and embrace. If they would but read the book, surely their eyes would be open to the truth, and their doubts removed.

The silence was broken by the eldest, the last of the original council; one most had forgotten was one of the first dwarfs in Hozekan, as he was an introvert. In a slow, raspy, kind voice, Falinn Viden spoke, "May I please see the book, dear Wiltzer?"

Wiltzer stood and handed Falinn Viden King Salvare's *Book of Wisdom*. For a moment, Falinn Viden focused only on the title, holding the leather book firmly with both hands. Laying it on the table in front of him, he softly ran his hand across the cover. All watched him as he opened the book. He slowly turned the pages as if searching for something he knew was there. Noting a place in the pages with his pointer finger, he moved it along as he read.

"Fear not my little children. I must needs go to my father but for a little while. Though the darkness shall come, and shall take prisoner all of those who reject the truth, ye shall be a light unto them. Fear not when the darkness surrounds you, for you will not be overtaken, for even in death you are freed from its grip. Love one another, that ye may be comforted during the tribulations of this life. Forgive one another that ye may be able to love with a pure heart. When darkness comes, for even now it worketh, and the wicked one which brings it, shows his scarred face, which was given the deadly wound, but was healed by the dragon, know that it is the time of which Judarius spoke of the *Ekleipsis*.

"Fear not, for it will be but for a moment, yet flee to the place of hiding which shall be told you. Wait for my witnesses there, and then shall the daystar rise high above the darkness. Then shall I return with the glory and power of my father, and with my faithful servants of the ages. Ye shall see me coming and I shall quench the darkness from before the eyes of Erde. Then shall I bring you to New Erde, and ye shall be my people, and I shall be your king. Faint not dear children, for you are forever in my heart and on my tongue to my father. I go to prepare you a place, whereby we may dwell, free of the darkness, forever."

No one spoke. Shock filled each soul as they pondered the words, and wondered how Falinn Viden seemed to know they were there. For none of them had ever laid eyes on such a book, nor heard these words read. It seemed as though the reading of those words had stirred the hearts of the emperor and council to consider what Wiltzer had told them.

"It has been a long time since I have read these words, for I had all but forgotten such truth existed outside of Hozekan." A tear escaped his eyes, dripping down his cheek, and falling to the page below. "My friends, there are no truer words, and the time is upon us."

Falinn Viden looked up, "Forgive us my people, for in trying to hide us from the *Darkness*, it seems we have also kept you from the truth."

# Unrest in the Land of Erde

*M*ighty unrest now resided in the land of Erde. Trachten, the Land of the *Seekers*, had been attacked and overrun with *Gottlos* and *Ubils*, with the setting up of the image by Jagare. Dartego's last word was a warning to Ciafus and the *Sealed*, at Kirche, of the coming *Ekleipsis*. Nesal had been attacked from within by Labo, carrying both the *mark* and the weapon of the *Darkness*. Vandor and Kayla rushed toward Trachten in search for his grandfather MaZak, and onward to Signum to speak to the *Sealed*, while recently-met Wiltzer and his wife, warned their dwarf brothers and sisters in Hozekan.

## § *Trachten* §

Trachten, the Land of the *Seekers*, the place where the inhabitants of Erde visited twice a year, to enquire into all that was new and different, was overwhelmed with disgust. Large, brute beasts, namely *Gottlos*, had taken captive all who had survived the rampage of *Rubicund* and their attacks. The *Gibborims* were there, awaiting the order to be given by their brother Jagare, as to grant them permission to wreak havoc throughout all of Erde, at their pleasure.

In Palvolin, of Trachten, a great image was raised, set there by Jagare, which towered above all the buildings of Erde. The iron *Dragon*, covering the core made from the clay of *Oscuridad*, was overlaid with gold. It stood massive upon its muscular legs, with its wings extended from side to side, head raised high with open jaws, showing its fierce teeth. Its tail sat on the ground, curling around to the front of its body, where the image continued with a golden plated, iron Jagare standing strong, driving his sword into the heart of King Salvare's *Book of Wisdom*, beneath his feet.

Jagare stood facing the image with his brothers. His arrogance overwhelmed his soul, for he was proud, beyond measure, of his image. His desire was to conquer with the sword, that at his name, of all that dwelt in Erde, every knee would bow, and every tongue would proclaim him as their majesty. There would be no mercy for the soul that dared not fall down, and worship at the feet of the image, and confess Jagare, King of Erde.

"My brothers, the time has come for you to bow down to the image, which I have set up. For, in this image, shall we conquer Erde, and bring every soul under obedience, to their new king. I shall be the almighty king, and you shall serve me as my right arm." Jagare turned to face his brothers, all but Desgosto, which he slew aforetime. "At the sound of the chants of the *heks*[f] of *Oscuridad*, may each soul pay reverence to the image, or endure the fire of the *Dragon*."

At the rising of the sun, reaching noon, the *heks* began their chants. The sound of harmonic hums could be heard in unison, with unknown tongues. The smooth, soft sound gradually increased to a constant octave of medium tone. It was simple, yet hypnotizing, seeming to move within one's mind and spirit.

"Jagare, have you gone mad? What needs do we have with an image to bow down to, and the silly chants of these witches?" questioned Abejoti. "I have doubts these things will serve us any purpose in bringing the people of Erde to grabble at our feet."

[f] a female witch, user of dark magic and sorcery

Jagare turned in disgust, "Why must my own blood doubt and defy me at every turn? Shall I be worshiped by Erde if my own kinsmen do not treat me with due reverence?" Snarling in anger, he cried, "*Rubicund*, come forth!"

From behind them, opposite the image, came forth the magnificent beast. He had been there all along, merely hidden from the eyes of the persons he watched. His power was unknown, his strength unmatched, his countenance feared. Standing above the height of the image, fiercer than any image can portray, he covered the sun, causing a shadow to drape around Jagare and his brothers.

Jagare's brothers tensed and held their stance still. None dared to move or speak, as the *Dragon* towered above them. With smoke flowing from his large nostrils, and the rumbling of the furnace within his bosom, his large emerald eyes sparkled, focusing directly upon Abejoti. The other brothers sensed this, and slowly stepped backwards, ever so lightly. As the *Dragon* lowered his mighty head, their pace increased.

Abejoti turned to Jagare, as the *Dragon* drew nigh, "Have you no mercy for your own blood?"

"I no longer share blood with you, dear Abejoti; for my blood doest come from the *Dragon*, and in that blood do I have life and power."

With that said, Abejoti looked back to the *Dragon* to meet his end. The flames from the jaws of *Rubicund*, the beast from Kriminala Pasaule, of whom little is known, but much is feared, engulfed Abejoti. His cries could be heard over the chants of the *heks*, and though these brothers were mighty men, chills still raced down their grimy muscular backs.

Jagare turned to the brothers, lamenting not over what had just transpired, "Cry not for Abejoti, for I have sent him to the bowels of Erde, to be tormented with Desgosto. Tell me this day, whom will ye serve? Will it be self or will it be King Jagare?"

The brothers voiced their obedience to Jagare. "Well then, hear ye not the sound of the *heks*? Bow down to the image which I have set up, and prove your allegiance to King Jagare of Erde."

Obedience was followed by the brothers. Today was but the beginning, whereby all of the *Gottlos*, the *Gibborims*, and servants of the *Darkness* bowed the knee to Jagare of *Oscuridad*. They professed him as King Jagare of Erde, swearing obedience, and receiving the *mark*, if by chance, they did not already bare it. This day was for the servants of *Darkness*, but tomorrow and hence forth, it would be the fate of all that dwelled in Erde.

§ *Signum* §

In Signum, inside of Kirche, the *Sealed* met to assess the concerns of the recent knowledge of the Land of the *Seekers*. Word had arrived from villages around Trachten, that indeed, there was a great army dwelling there. News of small *Gottlos'* groups tormenting some of the neighboring villages, taking their maidens and children, except for those able to hide, and slaying anyone who opposed them, was also brought forth.

The council room was full, front to back, elbow-to-elbow stood men and women of the *Sealed*. Those who were currently in Signum, and those notified from the surrounding villages had gathered there, at Kirche, to hear the words of Ciafus, the Auctoritas. The air was full of voices of the current stories concerning Trachten, the *Gottlos*, Jagare and his brothers, and the *Ekleipsis*, along with ideas and thoughts as to what should and should not be done. Even as they mingled there, there were those of the *Sealed* which were presently moving to warn the people of Erde, to tell them what they needed to do, and to where they needed to go.

As Ciafus entered the room, silence began to ripple through the crowd. He took his seat at the table with the council, which had been pushed to the far end of the room, being there were not enough chairs to accommodate all of the people. To the rear of table, there behind Ciafus, mounted to the wall, was a large map of Erde, with a red marking located near the top north east portion, that most taking note of, had never seen. A large copy of King Salvare's *Book of Wisdom* lay upon the table, in front of Ciafus. Next to the *King's* book sat a smaller book, having the cover engraved with 𝕲𝖊𝖍𝖊𝖎𝖒 [f].

§     §     §     §

"Geheim" was not a word used by the people of Erde, nor was it a term that many had ever heard. In fact, it was both a name and a place which had been hidden well, since the departure of King Salvare to Himmel, the kingdom of his father, King Allmachtig, many years ago. It had been a well-guarded secret, known only to the Auctoritas, the council, and the souls who had chosen to work and live in Geheim, since the beginning.

Geheim was created as a place of refuge, for the people of Erde, from the *Darkness*. It dwelt to the east of Signum, along the Liban River, through the Ascuns Forest, past Nesal and Breckenly, deep into the Cadas Mountains, nourished by Lake Szikla. The *Great Awakening* came before it was stable enough for the inhabitants of Erde, but it had since been strengthened and supplied, if ever there were a need, for Jagare and his brothers to live.

§     §     §     §

Ciafus addressed the people, "Dear Council and *Sealed* of King Salvare, it appears that the time of the *Ekleipsis* is indeed at hand. Witnesses around the Land of the *Seekers* have yielded clear evidence of a mighty army of *Gottlos* stationed there, along with the *Dragon*, known as *Rubicund*. We have dwelt in a shadow of peace since the falling of Jagare, but now that shadow wishes to pull us into the *Darkness*. The time has come to share with all of you the secrets, which those who watch over your souls have thought it best to keep hidden, for

---

[f] meaning 'secret'

the sake of protecting the people of Erde."

Ciafus opened the *Book of Wisdom*, as he continued, "As you should all well know, King Salvare did proclaim, 'When darkness comes, for even now it worketh, and the wicked one which brings it, shows his scarred face, which was given the deadly wound, but was healed by the dragon, know that it is the time of which Judarius spoke of the *Ekleipsis*.'"

Looking up from his reading, and taking hold of the book, entitled 𝕲𝖊𝖍𝖊𝖎𝖒, Ciafus declared, "Today I must tell you of the place called Geheim, and we must move at once to warn the people of Erde, to move them to safety. It is at Geheim that we must wait, for it is written, 'flee to the place of hiding which shall be told you.'"

Turning through the pages of the *Book of Wisdom*, he continued reading, "When the darkness of the wicked one shall come, and the shadows shall seem to block out the light, flee from the sounds of mesmeration[f]. Take not the *mark*, nor kneel to any image, but run to the land where the dragon cannot fly. But stay not there, for it will only keep thee for but a time. Continue past the regions of knowledge, that you may be covered by the hand of Erde, and nourished by her tears."

Once again, staring out across the people, Ciafus proclaimed, "Dear brothers and sisters, we must move the people of Erde, that still give allegiance to King Salvare, and who have not taken the *mark* of the *Wicked One*, to Geheim. Geheim lies through the Ascuns Forest, where the *Dragon* cannot fly, and into the Cadas Mountains, whereby Geheim lies outside of the knowledge of Erde. There, covered by the mountains, the hand of Erde, we shall be nourished by Lake Szikla, her tears."

A voice from the crowd asked abruptly, "And how long do you suggest we stay there Ciafus? How long do we believe Jagare will not discover such a place?"

[f] to be mesmerized by; hypnotic

Ciafus flipped back the pages, finishing the previous passage, "'Wait for my witnesses there, and then shall the daystar rise high above the darkness. Then shall I return with the glory and power of my father, and with my faithful servants of the ages. Ye shall see me coming and I shall quench the darkness from before the eyes of Erde. Then shall I bring you to New Erde, and ye shall be my people, and I shall be your king. Faint not dear children, for you are forever in my heart and on my tongue to my father. I go to prepare you a place, whereby we may dwell, free of the darkness, forever.'"

Murmuring filled the room, echoing loudly against the acoustic walls. Disagreement, questions, belief and unbelief, found themselves clashing one against another, failing to listen to what was heard, along with faith, logic, understanding, and opinions facing off for battle from each individual.

"Quiet!" shouted Ciafus, to regain order. Heads turned, as silence was reached once again. "Dear people, 'Fear not when the darkness surrounds you, for you will not be overtaken, for even in death you are freed from its grip.' We are told to, 'Love one another, that ye may be comforted during the tribulations of this life. Forgive one another that ye may be able to love with a pure heart.' My friends please take heed to what the council has to say. There is much that must be done."

§ *Nesal* §

In Nesal, as the bright warm sun broke over the trees, the sad songs of the night had transposed into vengeful thunders and lightings. The village was enraged by the actions of Labo, for now there were wives left without husbands, and children without fathers. The death of Labo was not enough, for the people cried out for more blood. They had searched for hours to find Sycress, Labo's wife. If it would not have been for the dogs, she may very well have hid beneath her home till night to escape. The people demanded answers, of which she claimed to have none.

Two men held Sycress by the bell, which Nau had rung merely hours ago, while women of the village screamed out, demanding that she be put to death. Cries of, "burn the witch" and "kill the wife and mother of devils" could be heard from the mouths of some of the most thought-to-be chaste ladies in Nesal. Rumors of her *marked* husband and sorcerer son were violently being used against Sycress, as she wept and continued to deny to have had any knowledge of either.

Nau, along with his wife, scarcely observed the vile words being spewed in the village, as Amashai pulled Hisum and Misal tightly to her. She buried their faces into her dress and tried to cover their ears with her hands. Sorie stood there, along with Eslar, failing to understand why her husband Tindal was even giving ear to such desires of the people. Sorie was grieved and somewhat frightened by the recent deaths, yet she could not conceive how the lack of mercy, toward Sycress, would bring comfort back to Nesal.

The people were demanding that Sycress be burned at the stake, as a witch. The law indeed gave authority to the council to hear such matters, and to execute punishment where necessary. The problem lied not with the law and punishment, but with the hearts of the people and their thirst for vengeance, without first allowing the matter to be heard. There was no council, thus the people were restless. There was no one left to punish, only Sycress in their eyes, and Tindal seemed eager to hand her over to the people.

From the back of the crowd, pushing his way to the front, moved an elderly bearded man wearing a tan cloak. Carrying a straight smooth wooden staff, with his face covered by the hood, he moved effortlessly between the screaming men and women. Standing between the crowd, before Tindal and the two men holding Sycress, the man slid back his hood, exposing his piercing eyes. The bearded man was Ashvar, and Tindal was most surprised to have the *seer* appear at this most inopportune time.

Standing in front of all of Nesal, Ashvar directed his thoughts to Tindal, "What is it thou doest, dear Tindal? Has your heart been seared, by the cries of the people, that you can see only law, without mercy? Are you ready to condemn a soul before the matter can yet be heard? Do you now hold the high office of the council, one that is to be a just man to the people, yet have allowed them to persuade you to do that which is unjust, and against such law you claimed to uphold? Do you yet convict her within thine heart, because you are angry at another? Are your thoughts so clouded that you are unable to recall that which you have been taught, by the wise men of old? Shall the laws of Nesal and the *Book of Wisdom* be laid aside, so that the people and their judge may have their unruly lusts fulfilled?"

He paused, and with no response from Tindal or the crowd, continued, "Give not this woman over to death, for she is indeed innocent of the crimes of which she is charged. Shall the mother be punished for the sins of her child, or a wife for the sins of her husband? Let it not be so, for let every man be judged and punished for their own sins. For he that judgeth his neighbor by another man's sins, let him also be judged by the sins of another."

Turning to the people, Ashvar continued, "Do not forget mercy and grace, as you mourn, and desire judgment against the wicked. For, would we not desire the same if we shall find ourselves within their grasps? Today I have come to warn the people of Nesal of the coming *Ekleipsis*, which lies but over the horizon in Trachten. There is much we must do, for the armies of *Darkness* do now prepare to destroy all light from the land of Erde. Prepare yourselves, you people of Nesal, for the *Darkness* cometh upon us. Let it not overcome your mortal bodies nor steal your souls, but let us dwell in the light finding ourselves to be good and faithful servants to King Salvare and his *Book of Wisdom*."

# Separated Hearts

*V*andor and Kayla finally arrived on the far outskirts of the Land of the *Seekers*, after being warned by passing villages, of the *Gottlos* attacks and armies dwelling therein. They had traveled a great distance from Nesal, and were somewhat worn. They had seen many people and places which they had never laid eyes on before in Erde. Many things were new to them, and would have held their attention more if the desire to find MaZak had not overwhelmed all their senses.

As they beheld the view across the horizon, their eagerness to rush into Trachten, to find MaZak, was somewhat softened by the sight of troops, like ants covering the landscape before them, in the distance. The foes of *Darkness* seemed to number greater than told.

For a moment they gazed into the distance, at a bright light that shone near the southwest portion of Trachten. Flames seemed to blaze from the same location, and then vanished. Reality seemed to come to terms within their mind. How to get into Trachten without being noticed, where to look once there, how to escape after MaZak was found, and countless other thoughts rushed wildly through their imaginations. They had considered none of these things while rushing off foolishly into the great unknown.

Closer to them, to the north, they noticed the kicking up of dust, which appeared to be some type of small struggle between a number of persons, on either side. Taking note of the glimmering coming forth from the armor of some, Vandor and Kayla assumed they were numbered among the *Sealed*, and the larger fellows, of which they contended, must be *Gottlos*, or at least servants of the *Darkness*. They pricked Korb and Dove with their heels, and made advancement toward the fight.

The closer they got, the more brutal they saw the combat was. Indeed, they saw those who wore the shining armor of King Salvare. Most of the men appeared to be in their forties, with one, maybe but a few years older than Vandor and Kayla. The elders used their swords against the large *Gottlos* with grace. The younger seemed to hold well his stance, yet his fundamentals were not as refined.

Vandor and Kayla dismounted near a large fallen tree. Vandor drew his blade, while agreeing that Kayla could use her bow from there. For a moment, they simply stared at the beasts, which fought the *Sealed*. The moments by the stream, with Rayhold and the *Gottlo*, filled their minds with pictures so vivid, as if they found themselves there but again. Anxiety desired entrance into their hearts. Pushing against it, they refused to stand idle by the way.

Rushing forward into the brawl, to the back of the foes, Vandor ran his sword into the side of one of the *Gottlos*, fighting the younger *Sealed*. Flinching, the *Gottlo* turned and slung his blade toward Vandor, grunting in discomfort. Raising his blade to block the *Gottlo's* blow from his face, the force was too strong for one arm, and knocked Vandor to the ground. Quickly, Vandor sliced the calf of the *Gottlo*, and then rolled, recovering himself to his feet. The *Gottlo* was struck by an arrow in his left shoulder, which held his sword, followed by another in the center of his back. He fell to his knees, as Vandor wasted no time piercing through the *Gottlo's* stony heart with the blade his grandfather had given him.

The *Gottlo* had fallen forward with dead weight upon the sword. It took a moment for Vandor to roll over the heavy foe to withdraw his weapon. Looking over his shoulder, he could see three more *Gottlos* running toward them, from the direction of Trachten. "Three more!" he shouted, as he made his way to battle another one of the *Gottlos*.

The battle raged on, with Kayla running low on arrows. She knew she must be more sparing with her shots, watching mostly for care of Vandor. She could see the fatigue growing within the men of the *Sealed*. Sweat rolled down, following the contours of their faces, burning their eyes, as they contended against the foes of *Darkness*. Continuous blows against their blades, jarring their clinched grips and tightened muscles, gave way to exhaustion with every assault. Four *Gottlos* were dead, leaving three showing no signs of retreat, with two of the *Sealed* lying lifeless, having gone on to meet their *Maker*.

The younger of the *Sealed* had fallen beneath the mighty blows of the *Gottlo*. Vandor took notice from the corner of his eye, and knew he was the closest. Turning from his foe, he fought against fatigue with every fiber of his being, forcing himself toward his fallen comrade. Kayla released an arrow, which silently pierced between the eyes of the *Gottlo* of which Vandor had just fled. The *Gottlo* fell to the ground, twitching but for a moment.

Kayla, keeping her eyes fixed on Vandor, reached to find another arrow. The quiver, across her back, felt empty. She turned to look, finding one yet remained. Pulling it forth, she slid it into place, resting it upon her hand which held the bow, slowly drawing it back against the string. She focused on the *Gottlo*, which stood over the fallen *Sealed* raising his sword to slay the young man. She feared Vandor would not reach him in time. She steadied herself, and controlled her breathing. As her drawn fingers loosened, to release the arrow of hope, she was struck in the back by a mighty force. She felt the arrow slip from her finger tips, and as her eyes closed, she fell unconscious to the ground.

Hearing footsteps from the *Gottlo*, Vandor's hand released his sword, refusing to grip it any longer. He watched it fall to the ground in disbelief. Vandor screamed in pain as the disrupted arrow buried itself within his right shoulder. Vandor turned in Kayla's direction. Unable to stop moving forward, the force pushed him almost over, causing him to stumble. The *Gottlo* was caught by surprise. It turned, swinging his sword toward Vandor, more as a club than a blade. Vandor's head was met with tremendous force of the flat portion of the blade, jarring every member of his being. Vandor clasped to the ground as if dead, but this gave the young *Sealed* the opening to pierce the *Gottlo's* heart.

The young man saw two *Gottlos* upon horses, striding toward Trachten, from whence Kayla was. One had Kayla in front of him, laden across the saddle. The other screamed words, unknown to him, in a seemingly animal dialect, that sent chills down his spine. The *Gottlos*, which the *Sealed* fought, turned and ran toward the others upon horseback. Burdened, the men let them go, without strength to follow.

The men fell to the ground, dropping their swords, sitting and catching their breaths. Removing their helmets, they bent over staring at the ground. The young one, whom Vandor had rushed to help, moved slowly over to check for signs of life. Had he lost this friend, before ever getting to know him? *He's alive!*, he screamed within himself.

The men, including Vandor, were dirty, covered in blood and sweat, mixed with tears and dust, their bodies full of bruises. Although they would all live, *what of the young girl who accompanied my new friend?*

# Rally in Geheim

*I*n Trachten, the *Gibborims*, the remaining sons of Galtare, along with Vikadore, divided the armies of *Darkness* to cover the land of Erde. With the loss of Desgosto, then Abejoti, the brothers' thoughts of tyranny, for the souls of Erde, had only increased. There was not a soldier of the *Darkness* which did not bare the *mark* 🌀, and that had not bowed a knee in reverence to King Jagare and his image.

The *Gibborims*, *Gottlos*, and *Ubils* were all ready to move at the voice of Jagare. Their thirst for blood drooled down their faces, like ravenous wolves. *Rubicund*, the *Dragon*, towered above the armies, staring across the land of Erde, able to see for miles past Trachten. Concerning the inhabitants, there seemed to be very few, which the *Dragon* could not see, for he had long moved about, seeking whom he may devour.

§    §    §    §

Kirche had been cleared out, with only a few yet remaining, to make one last sweep, to gather what may have been left of importance. Mere handfuls of people still made their way through Signum, as they refused to leave their belongings behind. Loaded down donkeys and wagons could be seen moving throughout the city, with but a few of the *Sealed* holding out for the stragglers, to lead them to safety. Their love of, and refusal to depart with, their possessions, had caused them to be left behind by Ciafus and the Council of Kirche, along with many others, who had chosen to leave such belongings.

At this very hour, while the souls of Signum arrived in Geheim, there were many among the *Sealed* which protected their backs from threats that arose from Trachten. A good number of the *Sealed* searched the grounds of Erde, warning and persuading men, women, and children to follow them to safety, from the coming menace of the *Darkness*. There were many which followed, those who mocked, and others who claimed they would be on their way shortly.

§     §     §     §

Persuaded by Ashvar, the majority of persons in Nesal had safely made their way into the hidden parts of the Cadas Mountains, called Geheim. Met there by persons of Ashvar's own village, Breckenly, and villages from all around the land of Erde, there must have been thousands upon thousands of men, women, and children arriving throughout the day. Seeing the insignia of King Salvare upon the many *Sealed* present, gave comfort to the weary.

Sycress, Rayhold's mother, refused to follow, but was permitted to stay with the few that chose to remain in Nesal. She wanted to linger there, in hopes that her son Rayhold would return. Sycress feared, if she were to leave Nesal, that her son might be lost forever to the *Darkness*; for how would he know where to reach the secret place of Geheim, on his own? Though she was not given the directions to Geheim, desiring to keep such from the approaching armies of Jagare, yet she remained, in hopes to see her son once more.

The first thing Tindal and Sorie did after arriving in Geheim, with the letter Vandor had left them in hand, was to inquire if any had seen their son. They were told to check the infirmary, for there were a few young men healing there. They made their way around the maze of people, while Ashvar moved to find Ciafus. Nau left his wife Amashai with his children Hisum and Misal, among the rest of the people mingling, as he followed Ashvar. Eslar accompanied Tindal and Sorie, in hopes to also find MaZak, though she feared, if he were yet alive, he would have returned to Nesal first.

Entering the infirmary, their eyes examined each face present, within seconds, looking for distinct details. There, toward the back, past more than twenty cots, laid their son, Vandor. Sorie gripped Tindal's hand tightly, as they made their way through the medical personnel. Eslar followed, taking a second glance at every face, hoping she may see MaZak or Dartego. She had asked for Ashvar to inquire of such, as he found his way to Ciafus, hoping he would return with good news.

As they reached Vandor, a lump still remained upon his brow, with his right arm held tight against his body with bandages. Sorie pushed past Tindal to her son. She knelt, allowing the tears to seep from her eyes, reaching out, placing her gentle hands upon her son's face. "Oh, my precious Vandor," she softly wept, kissing his cheek. Her tears dropped to his face, as he opened his eyes. Her heart leaped within her bosom, as she tightly embraced him. *Oh thank you, my God, for saving my son!*

Tindal smiled, kneeling and placing his hand upon his son's arm, "It is good to see you, son." A part of him groaned to demand Vandor give answers for his disobedience in leaving, and to question where and to what had he been about. The law dwelt deep within Tindal, but, for this precious moment of reunion, he refrained from allowing it to speak.

Sorie asked her son, "Is Kayla here?"

"No," Vandor said quietly, with a solemn look. "Are her parents here?"

"Tebad and Triamencia have stayed in Nesal to search for Kayla. Do you know where she is? We may be able to send them word," Tindal questioned.

"We came upon a battle in Trachten…she was taken by the *Gottlos*," Vandor began to tell, but was broken off by the arrival of his new friend from the battle.

A young fellow, with jet black hair and similar build as Vandor, approached. "This is Arkadas. He and others of the *Sealed* saved my life by bringing me here," Vandor proclaimed.

"Don't be so modest Vandor. It was you who risked your life to save mine, and helped us in the fight with the *Gottlos*. I only wish we could have been able to save your friend also," claimed Arkadas, showing remorse, speaking of Kayla.

Attention was drawn to the young girl, in the bed across the pathway, as she began to moan and shake drastically. She was strapped to the cot, across her shoulders and thighs. It was to protect her from harming herself, for she would spasm uncontrollably quite often. She remained in a comatose state, yet continued to sweat profusely, running a very high fever. The physicians had tried all that they knew, yet her condition only worsened by the hour.

Into the infirmary walked Ashvar, along with Ciafus and Nartod, the head physician of Kirche. They made their way to the convulsing young lady. Kneeling beside her, Ashvar bowed his head, placing his hands upon her arm and forehead. For a moment there was only silence, then her convulsions began to cease. Her sweat began to dry and her fever drifted away, as she appeared to begin to rest peacefully.

Ashvar looked up, as he removed the rose blossom necklace, which had now turned black, from around her neck. Crushing the amulet in his hand, he turned to Ciafus, "she has been touched by the *Darkness*."

Vandor reluctantly spoke, "She is Cenobia, from Qualtes." He did not want to tattle, but he knew he must. "Rayhold gave her the necklace."

He decided to tell them all of that which he had once kept secret. He gave record of going to Qualtes with Rayhold and Kayla, and while returning meeting the *Gottlos* and seeing Rayhold work magic. He revealed the secret that Kayla told him, of how her father, Tebad, also had one of the *marked* daggers of the *Wicked One*. He explained his desire to search out MaZak among Trachten, and how it led Kayla and him into the battle wherewith he was wounded and Kayla was taken prisoner.

Ashvar, Ciafus, Nartod, Arkadas, and his family, listened intently to all Vandor had to tell them. Some wished that they had known such beforehand, but it was too late to begrudge the young man when it was not done out of malice, and he faulted himself with such guilt already.

Ensuring Vandor was mostly finished with his story, Eslar could no longer contain her anxious heart, "Have you seen MaZak or Dartego," she questioned Ciafus.

Ciafus told Eslar what he knew concerning Dartego. He told of Dartego's accident, and his arrival in Signum, at Kirche, by the aid of Labat and his sons. Ciafus explained how Dartego had since passed away, yet gave warning concerning the coming *Ekleipsis* with his final breath. Nartod had done all that he could do, but Dartego had passed from this life to the next.

"Grandmother," Vandor said. "I met a dwarf named Wiltzer, who carried grandfather's sword."

Vandor continued, giving every detail he could remember about meeting Wiltzer and his wife Damaris. He told them of their old emperor Oviss, their new emperor Penuh Harap, and the place in which they lived, called Hozekan. Ashvar and Ciafus looked as though they had heard the names before, but they remained silent.

"Nartod," called a man from the entrance to the infirmary. Labat stood there with his two sons, Falken and Ion. With them stood a ragged young girl, with tangled auburn hair and heavy green eyes. Her clothes were tattered and blood-stained, as she stood at a distance from Labat and his sons.

"Kayla!" Vandor exclaimed excitedly, but her face remained emotionless.

Leaving her, Labat moved forward to speak to Nartod. "We found her wandering alone. She hasn't said a word, and she will not let anyone near her."

Vandor tried to get up from his cot. Unable to do so alone, Arkadas helped him to stand. Vandor walked forward toward Kayla, as Ashvar followed. Vandor stood before her, looking into her eyes, but she appeared to not recognize him. He looked down at her hand, taking notice she no longer wore the ring which he had given her. "Kayla," he spoke tenderly.

She stared at him oddly, taking notice of Ashvar, then turned, walking out of the infirmary, without a word.

Vandor was hurt beyond measure. If the thought of losing her were not enough, she was but found, yet was still lost to him. His heart hurt and burned to reach out to her, to hold her, to love her. The pain was more than a hundred arrows piercing his shoulder.

Ashvar placed his hand upon Vandor's unharmed shoulder. "The *Darkness* has been upon this one Vandor, and it may yet remain. Pray that God may grant us wisdom, and give mercy unto Kayla."

"She seems so different," replied Vandor with words that failed to be but an unrecognizable whisper of pain from the depth of his soul.

"Patience, Vandor. Your friend Kayla may yet return," Ashvar said to comfort him, before leaving the infirmary himself.

Ashvar found Kayla sitting alone, rocking with her arms holding her thighs against her chest, deep within the shadows of the crevasse of a rock.

The eclipse came forth, which no eye of Erde had ever seen. The armies of Jagare thirsted for it, the inhabitants of Erde feared it, and the souls in Geheim prayed to endure it.

# Ekleipsis

*T*he sign, of which Judarius spoke, now rested over the skies of Erde. The new moon moved, ever so softly, across the heavens, making its way to the forefront of the sun. Did it desire to claim all light for itself, or simply wish to withhold the sun's rays from reaching Erde? There was none who could stop it, for it moved upon the track whereby it was set.

The mighty roar of *Rubicund* sounded the call to the armies of *Darkness*, to prepare themselves for battle. The *heks* began their chants, and the *mark* upon the hands of Jagare's army, began to tingle beneath the flesh. The *Gibborims* and *Gottlos* freed their minds, giving themselves over to the sound of the *heks*, allowing the *Ubils* to indwell their beings. A union of *Darkness* and wickedness, baring record of the total depravity of such brute beast, brought forth unthinkable evil, which Erde had never seen. They went forth, spreading like a virus, to seize all of Erde.

*The sun seemed to stand still, shining bright, in all its glory. Did it not know that its heavenly friend, the moon, came to hide its countenance from the children of Erde? Could it not bring the heavens to a halt, or demand that the moon change its course, knowing it would bring forth darkness upon the people below? Did it not rule the day? Why did the sun yet remain silent and allow it happen?*

Fear began to infiltrate the very fibers of the persons which had remained in Erde, deciding against following the lead to Geheim. Candles and lanterns flicked throughout the villages, where people remained, waiting for the coming darkness. Some viewed the sky through their windows, while others braved the outdoors, sitting beneath the trees or against their homes. They waited to see the moon blot out the sun from among the heavens. Although they feared the darkness, they remained somewhat intrigued by it.

*Portions of light seemed to vanish, as the moon moved gradually across the face of the sun. Blotting the sun from the heavens, the darkness was inevitable. Eyes were blinded, as pupils tried to adjust to the lack of light. Though the darkness draped across all of Erde, the faint corona of the sun could yet be seen with the focused eye.*

Nyleve, one of the first ladies to live among the sustainers of Geheim, held her lantern and moved quietly toward a group of children gazing up to the sky. Dressed in a white gown, which flowed to the ground, she carried warm hazelnut muffins in a napkin-draped basket, to comfort the children. A delicate little girl sat among the slightly older children, with tears flowing down her freckled cheeks. Nyleve gently knelt beside the weeping child, and softly whispered, "Fear not little one, for the darkness is but for a moment, then shall you see the daystar shine again in all its glory."

Behold the *Darkness* cometh, upon the face of Erde, seemingly annihilating all evidence of light. Reaching out from the shadows, stealing the illumination, which yet remains surrounding them, demanding total submission, in claiming its dominance. The *Darkness* thrives on silencing the light, desiring to remove all remembrance of its being. Failing to realize light cannot be completely absorbed without limit, the *Darkness* gloats in its seemingly triumphant victory. All the while, the nimbus gives the souls of men hope, in seeing that the light yet shineth.

The *Ekleipsis* cometh but for a moment, then shall the daystar yet arise above the *Darkness*.

# Book Two:

## In the Land of Erde

*T*he *Ekleipsis* has brought forth death and *tribulation* more so than anything the souls of Erde could have ever imagined. The death records of the *Dark Ages* have far since been out numbered in mere months, since the night of the eclipse. Since the cry of *Rubicund*, the *Dragon*, upon the announcement of Jagare, the *Darkness* has not slept. It continues to go forth as a roaring lion, devouring the weak, the confounded, the faithless; all those who would not adhere to the call of wisdom to flee to Geheim.

On the night of the eclipse, Jagare sent forth his army across the land of Erde, to the sound of the *heks*[f]. This band of wickedness, which lay dormant in Erde for many years, was released to fulfill their lusts upon every living creature not subservient to Jagare. Led by Vikadore, along with the eight remaining *Gibborims* (Jagare's brothers, minus the slain Desgosto and Abejoti), the *Gottlos* swept across the land leaving no village unharmed. The *Ubils* followed among the shadows, infiltrating the minds of the frightened and lost.

Their total depravity was displayed in their slaughter of young children, their unnatural lusts and abuse toward women, and their inhumane acts toward the elderly and men of the villages. Unmentionable acts brought forth by vile affections, unseemly works, most horrendous atrocities were committed, and continue throughout Erde.

Moving across the land, these murderous beasts divided into bands. Baitrs and Pyktis moved their armies toward Kirche, in Signum, crumbling Xiacon along the way. Begeren and Ahnews marched through the higher regions of Erde, while Gniew and Hatan swept across the midlands, leaving Himo and Zolba to comb the south east portions. Vikadore remained in Trachten with Jagare as well as six hundred sixty-six *Gottlos*. With so much sorrow, the Erdians'[f] tears began to run dry, but their blood did not.

[f] a female witch, user of dark magic and sorcery

[f] the people of Erde

# Appendix

# Characters

Abejoti (A-be-jo-ti): Son of Galtare and third wife Vira. Brother of Jagare and twin of Ahnews.

Ahnews (Ah-news): Son of Galtare and third wife Vira. Brother of Jagare and twin of Abejoti.

Allmachtig (All-mach-tig): Father of King Salvare.

Amashai (A-ma-sha-i): Wife of Nau and mother of Hisum and Misal.

Arkadas (Ar-ka-das): Friend to Vandor.

Ashvar (Ash-var): Seer whom Sorie lived with after her family died.

Adevar (A-de-var): Youngest of the Council of Kirche.


-    B    -

Bailite (Bail-ite): Mother of Judarius.

Baitrs (Bait-rs): Son of Galtare and concubine Mayaton. Brother of Jagare and twin of Begeren.

Balor (Bay-lor): Thought to have killed Judarius.

Begeren (Be-ger-en): Son of Galtare and concubine Mayaton. Brother of Jagare and twin of Baitrs.

Bron van Vreugde (Bron-van-V-reug-de): Eldest of Council of Kirche.


-    C    -

Cenobia (Ce-no-be-a): Girl Rayhold likes in Qualtes.

Ciafus (Ci-a-fus): Commander of Arms of the *Sealed*.

Cohart (Co-hart): Member of the Council of Hozekan.

Damaris (Da-mar-is): Wiltzer's wife, which are both dwarfs.

Dartego (Dar-te-go): MaZak's friend.

Desgosto (Des-gos-to): Son of Galtare and second wife Essen. Brother of Jagare.

Dr. Toggle (Tog-gle): Doctor that delivered Vandor.

Ehrlich (Er-lich): Member of Council of Kirche.

Elinora (El-i-nor-a): First wife of Galtare, mother of Jagare.

Erdessest Kirche: (Er-dess-est Kir-che): Founder of Kirche.

Eslar (Es-lar): Mother of Tindal and wife of MaZak.

Essen (Es-sen): Second wife of Galtare, mother of Desgosto.

Falinn Viden (Fa-lynn Vi-den): Member of the Council of Hozekan, eldest.

Falken (Fall-ken): Labat's son and twin brother of Ion.

Fiken (Fi-ken): Member of the Council of Hozekan.

Frieden (Free-den): Member of Council of Kirche.

Fuerza (Fuer-za): Member of Council of Kirche.

Galtare (Gal-tare): Son of Judarius and father of Jagare and ten brothers.

Gniew (G-new): Son of Galtare and concubine Salena. Brother of Jagare.

Guesald (Guess-ald): Member of the Council of Hozekan.

Hatan (Ha-tan): Son of Galtare and concubine Karlami. Brother of Jagare and twin of Himo.

Hisum (His-um): Son of Nau and Amashai, and brother of Misal.

Himo (Hi-mo): Son of Galtare and concubine Karlami. Brother of Jagare and twin of Hatan.


- I -

Imbol (I'm-bowl): Member of the Council of Hozekan.

Ion (I-on): Labat's son and twin brother of Falken.

Ishbal (Ish-ball): Member of the Council of Nesal.


- J -

Jagare (Ja-gar): Grandson of Judarius and son of Galtare and first wife Elinora.

Judarius (Jew-da-ri-us): Son of Bailite, grandfather of Galtare, and betrayer of King Salvare.


- K -

Karlami (Kar-la-my): Concubine of Galtare, mother of Hatan and Himo.

Kayla (K-la): Vandor's love, daughter of Tebad and Triamencia.

Key (Key): Owner of Brocolate.

Kol (Coal): Member of the Council of Nesal.


- L -

Labat (La-bot): Falken and Ion's father, member of the Sealed.

Labo (La-bow): Rayhold's father and husband of Sycress.

Langmutig (Lang-mu-tig): Member of Council of Kirche.


- M -

Mayaton: (May-a-ton): Concubine of Galtare, mother of Baitrs, Begeren, and Zolba.

MaZak (May-Zack): aka The Bladesman, father of Tindal and husband of Eslar.

Misal (Mis-al): Daughter of Nau and Amashai, and sister of Hisum.

Nartod (Nar-tod): Head of medical at Kirche.

Nau (Na-u): Husband of Amashai and father of Hisum and Misal, and member of the Council of Nesal.

Nyleve (Ny-leve): Lady of Geheim.

Odvaha (Od-va-ha): Member of Council of Kirche.

Onyx (On-x): A pale that teaches Rayhold sorcery.

Oviss (O-viss): Previous dwarf emperor of Hozekan, father of Penuh Harap.

Pameten (Pa-me-ten): Member of Council of Kirche.

Penuh Harap (Pen-u Ha-rap): Dwarf emperor of Hozekan, son of Oviss.

Piradad (Pie-ra-dad): False seer, a pale, who brought Jagare back to life.

Pyktis (Pyk-tis): Son of Galtare and third wife Vira. Brother of Jagare.

Qad (Kaid): Member of the Council of Nesal.

Rakkaus (Rak-kaus): Member of Council of Kirche.

Rayhold (Ray-hold): Vandor's friend, son of Labo and Sycress.

Rubicund (Ru-bi-cund): aka Dragon, mysterious creature which some claim really controls the Darkness from Kriminala Pasaule.

Salena (Sa-len-a): Concubine of Galtare, mother of Gniew.

Salvare (Sal-vare): True King of the land of Erde, and son of Allmachtig.

Sir Trachten: (Trach-ten): Founder of Trachten.

Sorie (Sor-e): Mother of Vandor and wife of Tindal.

Sycress (Sy-cress): Rayhold's mother and wife of Labo.


-     T     -

Tamar (Ta-mar): Sorie's cousin, from Feltor.

Tebad (T-bad): Kayla's father and husband of Triamencia.

Tindal (Tin-dal): Father of Vandor and husband of Sorie.

Triamencia (Tri-a-men-c-a): Kayla's mother and wife of Tebad.


-     U     -

Usk (Us-k): Member of Council of Kirche.


-     V     -

Vandor (Van-dor): aka V, Tindal and Sorie's son.

Vikadore (Vike-a-dor): Caption of the Gottlos.

Vira (Vi-ra): Third wife of Galtare, mother of Abejoti, Ahnews, and Pyktis.

Vitis (Vi-tis): Member of Council of Kirche.


-     W     -

Wedgmark (Wedge-mark): Member of the Council of Hozekan.

Whisper (Whis-per): aka King Salvare's Whisper, a lingering of the King often felt by the Sealed.

Wiltzer (Wilt-zer): Husband of Damaris, which are both dwarfs.


-     X     -

Xima (X-i-ma): Governor of the Land of the Seekers, namely Trachten.


-     Y     -

Yanes (Yanes): Member of the Council of Nesal.

Zavest (Za-vest): Member of Council of Kirche.

Zoac (Zo-ack): Member of the Council of Nesal.

Zolba (Zol-ba): Son of Galtare and concubine Mayaton. Brother of Jagare.

# Groups

-     G     -

Gibborims (Gib-bor-ims): Name given to the linage of Judarius (specifically the children of his son Galtare). Jagare and his brothers are assumed to be heirs of the Darkness by the union of Judarius' mother Bailite and a fallen Malaikat (Ubil).

Gottlos (Gott-los): Evil creatures some claim used to be men that serve the Darkness, while others claim are half man and half Ubil.

-     H     -

Hek: A female witch, user of dark magic and sorcery.

-     M     -

Malaikat (Ma-lai-kat): Good spiritual messengers from Creator God.

Marked (Mark-ed): Name given to those that receive a mark after swearing allegiance to the Darkness.

Masonisti (Ma-son-is-ti): Those which claim to follow as the Sealed, but are most secretive.

-     P     -

Pale: A male sorcerer, user of dark magic, false seer, which is most often deathly pale in color.

-     S     -

Sealed (Se-aled): Name given to those who give their allegiance to the true king, King Salvare.

Seekers (Seek-ers): Name loosely used for those which are often looking for something new, especially during the markets of Trachten.

Seer: One able to see and proclaim the future (receives ability from God, contrasted to a pale)

- U -

Ubils (U-bills): Fallen Malaikat, once good but now evil spirits, which serve the Darkness.

# Places

- A -

Almozak (Al-mo-zak): Village south of Trachten where Sorie lived.

Ascuns Forest (As-cuns): Surrounds Nesal to its south and west.

- B -

Breckenly (Breck-en-ly): Village north of Nesal, where Ashvar lives.

Brocolat (Bro-co-lat) Inn: Common inn in Palvolin, Trachten.

- C -

Cadas Mountains (Ca-das): East of Nesal and Breckenly.

Cricket's Eatery: Restaurant next to Brocolat.

- E -

Erde (Er-d): The land in which all this is.

- F -

Felter (Fel-ter): Village where Tamar, Soric's cousin lives.

- G -

Geheim (Ge-heim): Secret hiding place within the Cadas Mountains.

Goslet (Gos-let): Village along the Liban River between Nesal and Salong.

- H -

Himmel (Him-mel): Kingdom of King Salvare's father, King Allmachtig.

Hozekan (Ho-ze-kan): *Sikwayi* village of the dwarfs, north east of the Lake Selatan.

Kartus Ocean (Kar-tus): North west ocean.

Kirche (Kir-che): Headquarters of the Sealed, in Signum.

Kriminala Pasaule (Kri-mi-nala Pa-sau-l): Where Rubicund the Dragon is from.

Lake Selatan (Se-la-tan): Lake south of Hozekan, fed by the Liban River.

Lake Szikla (Zik-la): Lake surrounded by the Cadas Mountains.

Liban River (Li-ban): River which flows from the Cadas Mountains.

Mount Dauthus (Dau-thus): Mountain on which Jagare resides in Oscuridad.

Nesal (Nes-al): Village south of Breckenly, where Vandor and family live.

Oscuridad (Os-cur-i-dad): Kingdom of Darkness, aka Darkness.

Palvolin (Pal-vo-lin): Area of the semiannual markets in Trachten.

Qualtes (Qual-tes): Village south of Nesal, where Cenobia lives.

Salong (Sa-long): Village at the Liban River, Umeten Canal connection.

Scimerian (Sci-mer-i-an]): aka Shimmering kingdom, kingdom of King Salvare.

Shadow Lands: aka Shadows, the lands before the kingdom of Darkness.

Signum (Sig-num): Location of Kirche, headquarters and training for the Sealed.

- T -

Telbaton (Tel-ba-ton): Village in Trachten, where Rayhold was from.

Trachten (Trac-ten): aka Land of the Seekers, settled by those desiring to serve neither King Salvare nor the Darkness.

- U -

Umeten Canal (U-met-en): Man-made canal from Liban River, which supplies Trachten with water.

- V -

Valtava Forest (Val-ta-va): The forest which protects and hides Hozekan.

- X -

Xiacon (X-a-con): Capital city of Trachten, where Xima and dignitaries live.

- Y -

Yoto (Yo-to) Inn: Dignitary inn in Trachten.

# Hidden Meanings

## The List

(Alphabetically)

| | | |
|---|---|---|
| Abejoti | "doubt" | Lithuanian |
| Adevar | "truth" | Romanian |
| Ahnews | "greed" | Finnish |
| Allmachtig | "almighty" | German |
| Arkadas | "friend" | Turkish |
| Ascuns | "hidden" | Romanian |
| Auctoritas | "authority" | Latin |
| Baitrs | "bitterness" | Goth |
| Begeren | "covet" | Dutch |
| Bron van Vreugde | "joy" | Dutch |
| Cadas | "rock" | Indonesian |
| Dauthus | "death" | Goth |
| Desgosto | "grief" | Portuguese |
| Ekleipsis | "eclipse" | Greek |
| Erde | "earth" | German |
| Ehrlich | "honest" | German |
| Falinn | "hidden" | Icelandic |
| Frieden | "peace" | German |
| Fuerza | "strength" | Spanish |
| Geheim | "secret" | German and Dutch |
| Gniew | "wrath" | Polish |
| Gottlos | "wicked" | German |

| | | |
|---|---|---|
| Gibborims | "nephilim" | Hebrew, Gen. 6:4, "mighty men." |
| Hatan | "hate" | Goth |
| Heks | "witch" | Norwegian |
| Himmel | "heaven" | German |
| Himo | "lust" | Finnish |
| Jagare | "destroyer" | Swedish |
| Liban | "living" | Goth |
| Kartus | "bitter" | Lithuanian |
| Kirche | "church" | German |
| Kriminala Pasaule | "underworld" | Latvian |
| Langmutig | "long suffering" | German |
| Mahla | "sap" | Finnish |
| Malaikat | "angel" | Indonesian |
| Morte | "death" | Italian |
| Odvaha | "courage" | Czech |
| Oscuridad | "the dark" | Spanish (Darkness) |
| Oviss | "doubtful" | Icelandic |
| Pameten | "wise" | Slovenian |
| Penuh Harap | "hope" | Indonesian |
| Pyktis | "anger" | Lithuanian |
| Rakkaus | "love" | Finnish |
| Rubicund | "red, reddish" | Latin, rubicundus |
| Salvare | "savior" | Late Latin |
| Scimerian | "shimmering" | Old English |
| Selatan | "south" | Indonesian |
| Signum | "seal" | Latin diminutive |
| Sikwayi | "sequoia" tree | Name of Muskogean man |
| Stejar | "oak" | Romanian |
| Szikla | "rock" | Hungarian |
| Ubils | "evil" | Goth |

| | | |
|---|---|---|
| Usk | "faith" | Estonian |
| Umeten | "man-made" | Slovenian |
| Valtava | "very large" | Finnish |
| Viden | "knowledge" | Danish |
| Vitis | "hope" | Lithuanian |
| Zavest | "knowledge" | Slovenian |
| Zolba | "malice" | Slovenian |

# The Light

## Council of Kirche

Auctoritas

("authority", Ciafus)

| | | | |
|---|---|---|---|
| Adevar | "truth" | Odvaha | "courage" |
| Bron van Vreugde | "joy" | Pameten | "wise" |
| Ehrlich | "honest" | Rakkaus | "love" |
| Frieden | "peace" | Usk | "faith" |
| Fuerza | "strength" | Vitis | "hope" |
| Langmutig | "long suffering" | Zavest | "knowledge" |

| | |
|---|---|
| Allmachtig | "almighty" |
| Himmel | "heaven" |
| Kirche | "church" |
| Salvare | "savior" |
| Scimerian | "shimmering" |
| Signum | "seal" |

# The Darkness

## The Gibborims

("nephilim", Sons of Galtare)

Jagare "destroyer" and his brothers (the ten kingdoms)

| | | | |
|---|---|---|---|
| Desgosto | "grief" | Himo | "lust" |
| Baitrs | "bitterness" | Abejoti | "doubt" |
| Begeren | "covet" | Ahnews | "greed" |
| Gneiw | "wrath" | Pyktis | "anger" |
| Hatan | "hate" | Zolba | "malice" |

| | |
|---|---|
| Dauthus | "death" |
| Gottlos | "wicked" |
| Kriminala Pasaule | "underworld" |
| Oscuridad | "the dark" |
| Rubicund | "red" |
| Ubils | "evil" |

# About the Author

The author dwells outside of the land of Erde within the boot of the United States. He works in the information technology field, while receiving joy by giving service to his church and writing when he can.

The author was saved by the Savior, Jesus Christ, on September 25, 1994. While serving in the U.S. Army, in Germany, the Spirit of God moved him to meet a Christian who attended a missionary's church for American servicemen. It was there that God the Father granted him repentance, and faith was placed in the Son of God, whereby the Holy Spirit quickened his dead spirit unto new life. His prayer is that all would come to know Jesus Christ as their Lord and Savior, and, for those who have, to act upon such convictions.

Please continue to visit www.landoferde.com to watch for updates and upcoming adventures *In the Land of Erde.*

www.ingramcontent.com/pod-product-compliance
Lightning Source LLC
Chambersburg PA
CBHW020434180626
46812CB00003B/1228